'[Piñeiro's] words work
masterful literature

'In Piñeiro's artful hands, each of her investigators learns
as much about himself or herself as about the murder
on the way to the surprising, perfectly executed ending.'
Publisher's Weekly

'Those willing to take the time to enjoy the style and the
unusual denouement will find themselves wondering why
more crime authors don't take the kinds of risks Piñeiro does.'
Booklist

'Piñeiro is AWESOME. Her books are dark, have buckets
of atmosphere (…)' —***Book Riot***

'Not for nothing is Claudia Piñeiro Argentina's most
popular crime writer.' —***The Times***

On ***Elena Knows***:

'Short and stylish…a piercing commentary on mother-
daughter relationships, the indignity of bureaucracy, the
burdens of caregiving and the impositions of religious
dogma on women.' —***New York Times***

'Her novels often feature incisive social and historical
scrutiny. (…) *Elena Knows* is a perfect example: a complex
character study of three women affected by their society's
oppressive rules, within a murder mystery.' —***The Guardian***

'A lyrical portrait of a woman unable to grieve…incisive
commentary on Catholic society's control of women's
bodies.' — ***Publishers Weekly***

Winner of
XII ROSALÍA DE CASTRO PRIZE
(Spain) 2014
For her literary career

Winner of
LIBERATURPREIS PRIZE
(Germany) 2010
For *Elena Knows*

Winner of
SOR JUANA INÉS DE LA CRUZ PRIZE
(Mexico) 2010
For *Las grietas de Jara* [*A Crack in the Wall*]

Winner of
CLARÍN PRIZE FOR NOVELS
(Argentina) 2005
For *Las viudas de los jueves* [*Thursday Night Widows*]

A LITTLE LUCK

First published by Charco Press 2023
Charco Press Ltd., Office 59, 44-46 Morningside Road, Edinburgh
EH10 4BF

A CIP catalogue record for this book is available
from the British Library.

ISBN: 9781913867553
e-book: 9781913867560

www.charcopress.com

Edited by Fionn Petch
Cover designed by Pablo Font
Typeset by Laura Jones
Proofread by Fiona Mackintosh

2 4 6 8 10 9 7 5 3 1

LOTTERY FUNDED

Claudia Piñeiro

A LITTLE LUCK

Translated by
Frances Riddle

CHARCO PRESS

To Ricardo, who isn't Robert but could be.

To Paloma Halac, who taught me where Mary Lohan comes from. And many other things.

To my children, Ramiro, Tomás, and Lucía. My biggest bit of luck.

This is acute pain. It will become chronic. Chronic means that it will be permanent but perhaps not constant. It may also mean that you won't die of it. You won't get free of it, but you won't die of it. You won't feel it every minute, but you won't spend many days without it. And you'll learn some tricks to dull it or banish it, trying not to end up destroying what you incurred this pain to get.

Alice Munro, 'The Children Stay'

Logbook:

The Return

The barrier arm was down. She stopped, behind two other cars. The alarm bell rang out through the afternoon silence. The red lights below the railway crossing sign blinked off and on. The lowered arm, the alarm bell, and the red lights all indicated that a train was coming. But there was no train. Two, five, eight minutes and still no train in sight. The first car drove around the barrier and crossed the tracks. The second car moved forward and took its place.

I should've said no, that I couldn't go, that it would be impossible for me to make the trip. Whatever excuse. But I didn't say anything. Instead I made excuses to myself, over and over, as to why, even though I should've said no, I agreed in the end. The abyss calls to you. Sometimes you don't even feel its pull. There are those who are drawn to it like a magnet. Who peer over the edge and feel a desire to jump. I'm one of those people. Capable of plunging headlong into the abyss to feel – finally – free. Even if it's a useless freedom, a freedom that has no future. Free only for the brief instant that the fall lasts.

Maybe it wasn't that I agreed to go simply because I didn't know how to say no; maybe, deep down, I truly wanted to. In some dark, private corner, tucked away so well I didn't even know it existed, was a desire to go back. It's even possible that I'd been waiting all this time for something to give me the push I needed. Into my personal abyss. Nineteen years. More: almost twenty. Waiting for something, or someone, some irresistible pull, some unavoidable circumstance to force me to return. Not my own decision because I'd never be able to make it. A decision made by destiny or by fate but not by me. To return. Not just to my homeland, Argentina, not just to the very city where I'd lived, Temperley, but back to Saint Peter's School itself. A return that, like some kind of Russian doll, ends in that miniature world: an English school on the southern edge of Greater Buenos Aires, a place I loved and hated with the same intensity.

Saint Peter's School. It's still hard to say the name, hard even to think about it. I know that the only person

I care about seeing won't be there. But maybe someone I knew, or someone who knew me. And him. Who knows about us from back when I still lived in that neighbourhood. Though the passage of time – and certain physical changes I've undergone – give me some peace of mind. I'm pretty sure I'll pass unnoticed. About five years ago, I crossed paths with Carla Zabala – one of the other mothers who was among my closest friends at that time in that place I'm now obliged to return to – and she didn't recognize me. It was in one of those superstores, we were both waiting in the checkout line, right next to each other. She looked at me and in very bad English asked if I knew the price of something she was buying. I was struck dumb, I couldn't respond. Carla waited a few seconds for me to answer, never registering who I was, and then simply asked the same question to the person behind me. That proved what I'd understood intuitively: I was no longer the person I'd once been. The person waiting in line in the superstore in Boston had never been to Temperley, never heard of Saint Peter's School, could never be recognized by Carla Zabala or anyone else, because she was a completely different person.

I don't even recognize myself when I look at pictures from that time. I only have three photos, all three of them with him, three different moments. None with Mariano. I hardly ever look at them now, I had to stop so that I could heal. It was Robert's suggestion and he was right. I kept doing it for a little while, in secret. But one night, when I was getting into bed, I realized that I'd gone all day without looking at them. And then two more days went by and I still didn't look at them. And then a week, a month. Time. Until I stopped looking at them altogether. But I never got rid of them. Now, today, on this plane that is returning me to the place I left behind, I carry four photos with me: those three plus one of me and

Robert, in front of our house. I don't look at them. But I still carry them with me, I don't even really know why.

I'm no longer blonde, like most of the women who sent their kids to Saint Peter's, that school I knew so well. For a long time now my hair has been reddish, almost ginger. I've lost weight, twenty pounds or more. I was never fat but after I left – after I ran away – I became emaciated, transparent, and I never regained the weight. I don't dress like those women, I no longer wear the clothes we all wore. Today, the day of my return, I look like an ordinary American woman, a Bostonian. If it were cold out I might wear a woollen hat, something unthinkable in Temperley. My voice, my old voice, will be hidden under my accent, which I'll make an effort to exaggerate. And it will be further distorted by the hoarseness that came into it the very day I left my country. 'Spasmodic dysphonia caused by traumatic stress,' said the doctor in Boston, several weeks later. Over the years it turned into chronic dysphonia from the strain placed on my vocal chords by the hours spent giving classes. Even my eyes are different. And not just because they've seen other things, other worlds. Not just because they never again looked upon the place I'm returning to today. If all that altered my gaze, the change would go unnoticed. Only I would be able to tell, maybe Robert too: a certain sadness, a dimness, a slowness in shifting from one object to another. Among those intimate changes, the place my eyes turn to search for words I can't find when speaking. I seek out my words on the ceiling; I stare up to one side and keep my eyes fixed there until the word finally comes to me. Robert stared straight ahead to gather his words, they were right there in front of him, always on hand; my mother – I now know – fluttered her lids. Where do his eyes go when he searches for words? I can't remember. But beyond any subtle shift, impossible to detect except by someone very attuned to my gaze, I've also made more obvious, external alterations. When my optometrist mentioned I could change my eye colour using special contact lenses, I jumped at the chance. Robert was shocked when he saw me. But Robert was incapable of disagreeing with me on anything, unless it was something that would harm me. So if I wanted brown eyes, I should have them. Robert. He liked my blue eyes. I didn't, not any more. 'Brown is perfect,' he said, despite his own preference. Meeting Robert, having his support when I moved to Boston of all the places in the world was like being thrown a lifeline in the exact moment I'd decided to abandon myself to the current and the waves, to let myself drift away.

I give Spanish classes in Boston. I teach Spanish to English speakers. First person or third? When do you use one over the other? These are some of the many questions my students ask once they get over the initial hurdles of the language and begin to write. The new students next semester will ask me again. It's a technical question and so that's how I respond to it – I give only grammatical answers, not literary ones – but this question in particular stays with me, as if it demanded a greater commitment from me. The students come to learn a language, the goal isn't for them to use this new language to write a novel or a story. That's what their mother tongue is for; a person should write in the language they use to think, the language they use to dream. The language that fills their silences. I know what my students expect of me and sometimes I feel like my answer is too theoretical: 'The person (first, second, or third) is a basic grammatical category, expressed using personal pronouns. It determines the concrete deictic form necessary to disambiguate the roles each interlocutor will occupy with respect to the predicate.' Deictic, disambiguate, interlocutor, predicate.

Bullshit, Robert would say. I can recite the definition from memory, I make the students recite it from memory. By heart, as we say. Memory versus heart. Sometimes I take pity on them and offer a friendlier answer: 'The first person is generally the person speaking: I, we. The second person is the person or persons they are speaking to: you. The third person is the person being spoken about: he, she, they.' And I, here, now, waiting to get on a flight back to Argentina, ask myself, as I stare at this page, if it would be easier to tell this story in the first person or in the third person singular. If it should be 'I' or 'she'. I try out one and then the other. The third person creates a kind of protective distance. The first person, on the other hand, pulls me to the edge of the abyss, invites me to jump in. I can hide behind the third person, stay two steps behind, avoid peering into that abyss even as I describe it. But I know that hiding is what I've been doing all this time. I haven't written so much as a single word about that day, about the days that followed, the years that followed. That's why I tell myself, will myself, force myself, to write this text – this logbook of my return – in the first person. Because that's the only way to describe the pain. Pain, heartbreak, escape, being shattered into a thousand pieces that can never be put back together, distance, abandonment, loss, scars, can only be narrated in the first person.

So I'm here in this New York airport. With Robert's help I was eventually able to get back on a train again and can now enjoy the beauty of travelling to New York by rail when there are no direct flights from Boston, so I can 'board the plane in a state of grace'. I sit waiting at the gate after checking a small suitcase filled with the things I'll need while I'm away, just over a week. And while I wait, I write, in the first person. I write for myself in the first person. I write myself. I'm calling

7

it a 'logbook' and not a 'diary'. Writing a diary implies some belief that your life is worthy of being recounted. The conviction that your life, as hard as it has been or is, deserves to be recorded day by day, scene by scene, from the perspective of the person who lives it. And I don't have that conviction.

I carry the photos with me. The four pictures. Robert's in front of the three older ones. If during the trip I have to look for something in my backpack and I come across them, I prefer to face Robert first, even now that he's dead and he can no longer protect me from my ghosts as he did all those years. First Robert, then him. In my backpack along with the photos is the paperwork I'll need to complete the task assigned to me by the Garlik Institute, the sophisticated American school I work for. I got the job as a Spanish teacher there thanks to Robert and there – swaddled in pain after running away from home – I began a new life. And that school is now flying me non-stop, business class, to another school, Saint Peter's.

Back to my past.

I place my backpack containing the paperwork and the four photos in the overhead compartment. There's plenty of room, business class passengers never have to use anyone else's allotted space. That's what they're paying for. I remove a few things from my purse before stowing it under the seat in front of me. I take out the book I'm reading, this notebook turned journal, as well as a pen, and a pack of tissues, and I put it all in the pocket of the seat in front of me beside the magazines and complimentary toiletry kit. I debate whether to take a pill, which would allow me to sleep at least six hours of the trip, or wait until the plane takes off, have a glass of wine with dinner, and hope the alcohol helps me doze off. I don't usually drink wine since Robert's been gone, so I expect one glass would have the desired effect. Even two glasses, or three, in business they'll do anything to please the passenger. I decline the champagne that the flight attendant offers, the bubbles tickle my nose and give me a headache. I take a pill from my purse and put it in the pocket of my blazer, in case I need it even after the wine. The plane must be about to take off. The empty seat beside me seems to be one of the few vacant spots left. Maybe, with a little luck, it'll stay empty. I don't have a lot of luck, like the kind my mother talked about. Meeting Robert twenty years ago might seem like the exception but that wasn't luck. It was one last chance placed in my path by fate, a choice between letting myself be led by the hand or letting myself die. The circumstances in which I met him, that's the kind of luck I have. Like now: a woman boards the plane carrying a baby and, luckily, she walks right past. Then a man. And another one. Until the flight attendant ushers an elderly woman down the aisle and sits her in the seat beside me, guiding her as if she were lost. The woman apologizes several times as she takes her place beside the window. She apologizes as if she'd done something wrong. She tells me that it's the fourth time she's ever flown on a plane, but the first time she's flown business. They upgraded her even though she didn't ask them to because there were no seats left in economy, which is the ticket class her son purchased for her. The first time she ever flew was for her son's wedding, alone, round trip. And now she's returning from a visit to meet her only grandson. She adds that it's just the two of them in the family, no one else. Her and her son. 'Now my grandson too,' she tells me, but she doesn't mention the daughter-in-law. She didn't have any problems on the previous flights, but she almost didn't make it onto the plane today, she tells me. She says this with resignation, not expressing any anger, as if she were describing some situation that's been imposed on her beyond her control, that she has no right to complain about. They sent her to the boarding gate with a blank space where her seat number should've been, explaining that they'd assign her one – if everything worked out – before boarding, and in the end the airline employees managed to upgrade her. And they said it with a smile: 'We've upgraded you.' Or I suppose those must have been the words they used because she tries to repeat exactly what they said but she can't remember, she closes her eyes and searches – just like my mother did. 'A word in English,' she tells me. And even though I'm sure they must've used that term, 'upgrade', I don't say it, I remain silent, on her side, the side of the woman who far from feeling like they did her a favour feels disoriented, annoyed in this seat with too many buttons, uncomfortable when the flight attendant asks her more than once if she'd like a glass of champagne. The anonymity afforded by economy class would've been more reassuring, no one fussing over her, offering her so many things and expecting her to enjoy them. The woman speaks as if she would've preferred her economy seat, even if she couldn't stretch her legs, arriving at her destination with swollen ankles, even if the food was worse, even if the child sitting behind her kicked her seat or her headphones were the only ones on the plane that didn't work. Those kinds of inconveniences were things she understood, she'd know how to adjust to them, or how to pass unnoticed while she suffered through them. These business-class inconveniences were foreign to her.

Sometimes, an upgrade only complicates life. That's how I felt when Mariano took me to live in Temperley. I'd lived all my life in Caballito, in a two-bedroom apartment: a small living-dining room, a bedroom for me, and one for my parents. And a terrace where my mother had plants, which always wilted because she forgot to water them, where my father read surrounded by wilted plants, and where I soaked up the morning sun. A rented apartment that was returned to its owners when my parents died, a few years after I moved out. Living in Buenos Aires seemed simpler to me, closer to everything, with more public transport. But Mariano had lived his whole life in the suburbs, in the home his parents inherited from his grandparents, an English-style town house with a garden and a small swimming pool against the back wall where a climbing rose grew. He managed his father's clinic – probably still does – which was only five minutes from the house. The only thing Mariano wanted, when he was looking for a place to live after we married, was to find a house as pretty as his parents', equally close to work. And he found it. He took me to see it one day without telling me where we were going. He untied the scarf I was wearing around my neck and used it to cover my eyes. 'Are we playing blind man's buff?' I asked. He helped me into the car, drove a few blocks, and parked. When he opened the passenger door so I could get out, I wanted to take off the blindfold but he told me to wait, that I would ruin the surprise. He helped me out of the car, guided me a few steps by the arm, stopped, let go, turned a key in a lock. Then we moved forward again over what I imagined to be a tiled walkway. A little farther on he stopped me again, turned me so that I'd be right in front of whatever he wanted me to see, and then he untied my scarf. I opened my eyes to a house in the same style as his parents' but much larger, better maintained, with a neater garden, more trees, and the same climbing rose but much fuller, on the front wall between the two windows. 'It's ours,' he said. I felt happy, but overwhelmed too. As if that whole house – which was going to be mine too – were leaning forward, about to topple over onto me. There had been no previous conversation, there was no joint home search. He chose what he thought best for the two of us, he decided for 'us'. Or for him. And for a while I felt like it was almost an undeserved gift. I thanked him, I felt like it was the best present he could ever give me. 'Proof of his love,' my mother said, 'you're so lucky, you don't know how lucky it is to have a house of your own, not to have to rent your whole life.' My father looked on but didn't say a word. At the time I thought that feeling of being overwhelmed meant something was wrong with me, it was my inability to receive what others wanted to give me, the trouble I had enjoying anything. Like that house, a house where Mariano and I could love each other, where we could be happy, where we'd start our family. A dream come true for any girl like me. Not my dream in particular, I didn't know what my dream was. So I appropriated the dream that other girls dreamed. After all, that dream wasn't a bad one, what more could I want in life. 'You're so lucky,' my mother said again that day as she had so many other times. And, so as not to contradict her, I agreed that yes, I was lucky, at least in a way. The kind of luck that keeps the lady with the baby from sitting down beside me. A little luck.

Before the plane takes off I quickly enter the address of that house into Google Maps. I count the number of blocks from the apartment where I'll be staying while I do my work at Saint Peter's – an apartment 'near the train station' it said in the email they sent with photos and the exact address, as if proximity to the station were some kind of advantage. I know that the flight attendant is going to ask me to switch off my phone and as I see her coming down the aisle I hurriedly trace possible routes from the apartment to the school without going past that house where we lived together for ten years. The best and worst years of my life. I'll be able to avoid walking right past it, it's just a question of taking the right street.

The flight attendant stops beside me and I tuck my phone away. The plane is about to take off. The upgrade lady, sitting to my right, squeezes her cross necklace with one hand and with the other, without asking for permission, she takes me by the arm. She shuts her eyes and prays.

I close my eyes too. I'm no longer thinking about Mariano, about the house, about Robert. I think about him, and about the routes he takes every day to go wherever he goes.

The barrier arm was down. She stopped, behind two other cars. The alarm bell rang out through the afternoon silence. The red lights below the railway crossing sign blinked off and on. The lowered arm, the alarm bell, and the red lights all indicated that a train was coming. But there was no train. Two, five, eight minutes and still no train in sight. The first car drove around the barrier and crossed the tracks. The second car moved forward and took its place. She waited, without moving into the empty space between her car and the one in front of her. She wondered whether that driver, too, was going to cross the tracks like the first one had. And as soon as she finished the thought, the car drove forward, manoeuvred around the barrier arm, and stopped. Although she couldn't see, she imagined that the driver was looking both ways to make certain no train was coming.

The pilot announces that we've begun our descent, the seatbelt light comes on, the flight attendants check that everything is in place, the seatbacks in their upright positions, the tray tables folded. Through the window, I watch as the darkness of the night is penetrated by the scattered lights around the airport. I hear the sound of the landing gear lowering and know that, beneath the wings, the wheels will now appear. I can't see them from where I'm sitting but I look to the flight attendant and her calmness confirms that the wheels are in fact there. I'm always attentive to these movements ever since Robert made me watch an episode of a Steven Spielberg TV show in which the landing gear of a bomber was broken, they'd lost a wheel, and they're only saved from the edge of death when a crew member draws in the missing wheel. A show with characters played by real actors – Kevin Costner is the captain – that introduces animation like magic so that the life-saving wheel can appear. If only changing reality were as simple as drawing a picture.

The plane is taxiing on the runway. The passengers applaud. Why do Argentine passengers clap when they land? I never saw anyone clap on any of the other flights I've taken over the years. The pilot applies the brakes and the plane begins to lose speed. I'm back in Argentina. After twenty years. But I haven't yet set foot on Argentine soil, my feet have only touched the floor of the plane. When can you say you've stepped back onto the land in which you were born? When can you say you have returned?

I stand up with a certain haste, though not as much as some of the other passengers who unbuckle their seatbelts and leap up before it's even allowed. I pull my backpack out of the overhead compartment and offer to help the woman who travelled beside me. She seems very grateful for the offer but something stops her from accepting and she says – almost embarrassed – that she's going to wait until everyone else gets off. She doesn't realize that business and first class passengers get off first. She doesn't care. Maybe she doesn't feel like she'd be able to keep up with my rushed pace. I'm not generally in a hurry. I lost my hurry a long time ago. Why rush? Where do I need to get so fast? Just the opposite, my everyday life centres around small actions aimed at helping pass the time, making it disappear into a series of unimportant motions completed without the slightest hint of urgency. After I fled home I never again felt rushed by anything. Or anyone. Robert respected my slowness, my total disinterest in the amount of time eaten up by any activity, conversation or wait. He declared himself in favour of slowness and said he admired my lethargy. I glance back at the woman before getting off the plane. She avoids my gaze, probably not wanting to feel questioned again. I think she would actually prefer to remain seated there until she's the only person left on the plane. She would choose, if she could, to pass totally unnoticed until the plane flies back to where it came from, back to her son's house. But she can't. Certain facts cancel out any possibility of regret. You can either act accordingly or not act at all. What you cannot do is change the facts.

I thank the flight crew and step off the plane, I cross the jetway, get in line at Immigration, show my papers, let them take one thumbprint, then the other, offer my face up to be photographed, wait for my luggage at the corresponding carousel. All this with a haste that is foreign to me. Maybe I would have preferred – like that woman – to stay on the plane until it took me back to where I came from, but, knowing I couldn't remain seated there, I decided I might as well get this whole ordeal over with as quickly as possible, pass this test and return to my life. That new life I built in Boston when I stopped being who I was before. The abyss attracts and repels me in a single motion. Like when we played tag as kids, we ran to catch someone and then immediately took off in the opposite direction. I return to my homeland, only to rush back to my adopted country. Quickly, as quickly as possible, immediately. But the game has not even begun because I don't yet feel like I've returned to Argentina. I didn't feel that I had returned when I crossed the jetway, or when I waited in line at Immigration, or in the toilets. Walking over this impersonal airport flooring, I still don't feel like I've stepped back onto Argentine soil. Is there any difference between the floor here at Ezeiza, at Logan Airport in Boston, or at Kennedy in New York? Or Barajas or Fiumicino or El Alto or Galeão. Identical cold tiled floors, interchangeable.

I stand beside the luggage carousel waiting for my suitcase to appear. In the distance I see the woman who sat beside me. She's looking for me, I'm certain. She glances all around. Finally she spots me and moves closer to where I'm standing. She stops a few feet away without saying a word, but it's clear that seeing me calms her. A familiar face, she must think. The guarantee that if I'm waiting for my suitcase at this carousel, hers must be about to pass by, any minute. She won't have to ask anyone. The woman, I infer, feels safe around me, protected. I watch her and I'm filled with a strange feeling, not unpleasant but kind of scary at the same time. I'm touched by the fact that this woman thinks she can rely on me. It's been a long time since anyone relied on me. I once knew how to take care of another person, how to hold them, rock them to sleep, remain attentive to every little thing they needed. But it's been ages since I felt that way, I never allowed myself to feel that way again. I even refused to get any pets – Robert would've loved to have a dog – just to keep from feeling that anyone in this world depended on me for survival. Robert didn't need me that way, just the opposite, in fact; he was the one who took care of me, soothed me to sleep, was always so considerate of my needs. He liked that role. And even though I knew it was unfair that I didn't take care of him in the same way, I simply wasn't able to. It was all I could do to let myself be cared for. Just that. Even that was a lot for the woman Robert met all those years ago on that flight to Miami, who fainted at his feet in the airport. What's strange about the thought that someone might rely on me – here in this airport – is not the fear it produces so much as the faint contentment that accompanies it, something like the sensation of waking up from a deep sleep. A resur-rected contentment: the satisfaction of feeling that you're needed by someone, necessary. A long-forgotten feeling, something I renounced long ago but can still recognize. After I ran away, I had to learn to accept that someday – sooner or later, once he got over it – he would no longer need me. His life would continue, like mine, and once he realized I was never coming back, whatever version they'd given him of the events and the reasons, he'd learn not to need me. His pain, a pain I can only imagine, weighs on me to this day, more than my own. My pain is still there but long repressed, flaring back up only when I think about his pain.

My suitcase has made it onto the belt. I wait for it to reach me, I collect it. I know that the woman is looking at me, worried that I have my luggage and she doesn't. I know it upsets her to see me rolling my suitcase towards the exit. But I don't turn around, I don't look back, I can't. I walk away and leave her behind, abandoned to her fate. It's not that hard to collect a suitcase. I fluff up my hair with my fingers, put on the non-prescription glasses that I wear when in addition to the coloured contacts I want another filter between my eyes and the world. I walk through the sliding doors and see a sign with my name on it: Mary Lohan. My name is María, María Elena, or Marilé. That's what everyone called me: Marilé. I now use Robert's last name, Lohan. 'You sure you want to have a last name that sounds like the airport?' Robert would say every time we took a flight. 'Mr Lohan flies out of Logan, how ridiculous.' I approach the driver who will take me to the apartment that Saint Peter's School has reserved for me in Temperley. The man offers to carry my suitcase and then takes it from my hand without waiting for my response. He wants to carry my backpack too but I won't let him. He puts my luggage in the trunk, we get in the car, he takes off. I close my eyes. I don't dare to look out the window for fear that some image might immediately trigger memories. I'm not ready to look yet.

After a little while on the highway I ask the driver to pull over. 'Are you feeling sick?' the man asks. 'Yes,' I lie. I get out of the car, take a few steps, remove my shoes, close my eyes. My bare feet on the grass. I wiggle my toes, shift my feet side to side with no intention of going anywhere. I only want to feel – not see, only feel – the rough grass scratching the soles of my feet.

Finally, I open my eyes.

Now I've done it.

I'm back, I have returned.

The apartment they've put me up in is nice. That's how I think of it, 'nice', a word I dislike. Nice is so lukewarm, it doesn't say much. But I can't think of a better way to describe it. Like when we say 'that's nice'. Polite, but lacking enthusiasm. A large living-dining room, a bedroom, a smaller room that serves as an office: shelves with a few neglected books, a desk with a computer and printer, an ergonomic office chair, a ream of paper, recently-sharpened pencils and a variety of pens in a coffee mug with the Saint Peter's logo on it, an adapter for different kinds of plugs sitting on the ream of paper. I expressly requested the computer and the printer since I don't like to travel with my laptop no matter how light it is. I prefer to download my files to a new computer in every place I go for work. Lugging my laptop around goes against something that for a long time now has felt like a necessity: travelling light.

The kitchen has an Italian coffee maker, a microwave, a toaster oven, and a full-sized fridge stocked with juice, fruit, cheese, milk, bread, frozen dinners. They've been expecting me. They've been expecting Mary Lohan, the American teacher sent as a representative from the Garlik Institute of Boston. They know who I am. Who I am now. The apartment seems to have everything I could possibly need to feel at home during my stay. It reflects the fact that whoever stocked it, or whoever sent someone to stock it, knows how to welcome a foreigner. They don't know that I'm not a foreigner.

As soon as we left Ezeiza, the driver gave me a message, or several messages: that first thing tomorrow morning, Mr Galván, the director of Saint Peter's School, would be coming by the apartment to pick me up, that Mr Galván apologized for not being able to meet me at the airport himself but that he wasn't able, given the late hour of my arrival. The driver repeated Mr Galván's name an excessive number of times and said again that he asked me to excuse him for not being there himself. More than excusing him I wanted to thank the man. I wouldn't have wanted a stranger to interfere with my homecoming after all these years. The driver is perfect: he only speaks when I speak to him first, he doesn't make any comments or ask any unnecessary questions, just responds to the few I make. With Mr Galván, it would've been different. He would've felt obliged to talk to me out of politeness, to ask me about the flight, if there had been turbulence, if I'd been able to sleep on the plane, if there was anything I needed. He might've even talked about work, tried to iron out a few details. When two people who barely know each other first meet, silences can feel unbearable, as if the air between the two bodies were heavy, I never understood why. Robert had it clocked, he said that after twenty-three seconds of silence between two people who don't know each other well, one of them will inevitably turn to small talk – the weather or even the taste of whatever they're drinking – not understanding that silence says more than anything either one of them could possibly say to avoid it. Even if you're tired, exhausted from travelling almost twelve hours, with nothing important to talk about, it feels more appropriate to speak – about anything at all – than to remain silent. Keeping quiet is frowned upon, it makes people uneasy. But I've been quiet for a long time, I'm comfortable with silence. I think I could go well beyond the twenty-three seconds of Robert's theory. The absence of enunciated words is my natural habitat, my default state, except when giving classes. And I think it's more awkward to blab about the weather just because whoever I'm with can't bear to go twenty-three seconds with their mouth closed. Maybe that's the true cause of my chronic dysphonia: social conventions force me to betray my natural silent state. Before I left Argentina, I'd never lost my voice and I'd never noticed that silence was the space I longed to inhabit. After leaving, I learned a lot about myself. The fact that I felt comforted by silence, for example. But luckily – thanks to my little luck – as well as my flight's late arrival time, Mr Galván couldn't be there to pick me up, to make sure that we never had to endure twenty-three seconds of silence.

The Garlik Institute, the school I work for, is prestigious and well-known not only in Boston but across the United States and Latin America. This prestige is based, above all, on the fact that students who graduate from our school can get into the best universities in the United States and Europe without much difficulty. It has one of the highest rates of acceptance to Ivy League colleges. This is thanks to the method Robert developed to prepare his students for success in college, a method that made him famous in the world of education. There was a time in which every single week he was giving a conference to explain his method to different schools around the country – his country, the United States. And for years, Robert, who was the director of the Garlik Institute until the illness kept him from getting out of bed, arranged educational cooperation agreements so that other schools, in other parts of the world, could become affiliated with our school and use our method – involving extracurricular programmes, teacher training, and other methods considered highly innovative in the educational sphere. I always tried to make Robert see that, beyond the fact that he and many other educators valued his method, some people – generally owners of private schools – would want to become affiliated with us regardless of the benefits to the students, simply as a stamp of quality, a framed certificate they could hang on the wall to reassure parents that the school was worth the expensive tuition. More aspirational than real: our name kept parents from questioning the level of education their child was receiving, made them empty their pockets without complaint. Even though Robert eventually realized that many schools in fact used the certificate more as a marketing ploy than out of interest in educational quality, the method was his pride and joy. He knew that it deserved to be shared and he never refused to consider any school that expressed interest. But he never granted the certificate to an institution that did not meet the established standards, that was not willing to make the changes asked of it, or that did not maintain educational quality over time – verified with an annual audit at the affiliated school's expense. The Garlik certificate could be revoked at any time by Robert – or by the person who's replaced him now that he's no longer here. When Robert received Saint Peter's request to be considered as an affiliated institute, he called me to his office immediately. He saw the name of the school and its location and he knew that so much of the person I'd been – and still was – had been forged there. He understood better than anyone what it meant for me to simply hear that name uttered. Although it would've provoked an ethical conflict, Robert could've made up some excuse to deny the request, without ever mentioning it to me. He could've avoided dredging up the past and setting it right down beside us. But he chose to face it, to face me, to tell me. Why did he spend so many years advising me to forget what had happened only to now do this? Because he was dying. Robert, by that point, knew about his illness. He knew that he was going to leave me alone and he wanted me to confront my past while he could still be there to hold my hand. But he failed to calculate one variable: time. He thought he had more life ahead of him. He was mistaken. That day, I pretended that it didn't matter to me what school was asking to be evaluated, that this school was just like any other and if Saint Peter's – I said the name, I couldn't remember how many years since I'd said that name – deserved it, Robert should of course grant them the certificate. I lied. Then I left. And we never spoke of the matter again. Then came the sudden worsening of his health, his death, the funeral, my two-week leave. I went back to work without a thought for Saint Peter's. Until the new director, Robert's replacement, called me into his office to tell me I'd been chosen to travel to Temperley, Argentina over the October break to evaluate a school. I asked the name of the school even though I already knew the answer. 'Why would you send me?' I asked. He didn't understand, of course, how could he: 'You are Argentine, aren't you? You could see relatives, friends...' Yes, I was Argentine, I am Argentine, but why would this man suppose I had friends or relatives there? And why did he suppose that, if I did, I'd want to see them? No, that wasn't the case. Generalizations and stereotypes don't always lead to accurate conclusions. I didn't say anything that day but I'd decided I would refuse. I wasn't going to tell the new director the reasons that kept me from going – returning. I didn't feel like telling my life story to that man or anyone else. Robert had known, and it had died with him. I would have to come up with some reasonable excuse. That day I missed Robert more than ever. I sat on the couch in front of the bookshelves where we'd spent so many hours, and, defying his blatant absence, I poured two glasses of wine, one for him, another for me. But Robert wasn't there, his glass went untouched. Days went by and the trip was never mentioned again. I certainly wasn't going to bring it up, so I just waited. But that was unwise. I should have been more proactive, taken the initiative, said I couldn't go. The abyss tugs at your heels. Then one morning they came to ask me about my plane ticket. If I'd rather fly through Miami or New York. If I wanted an overnight flight or a daytime one. If I preferred an aisle or a window seat. That's when I understood that my silence had been interpreted as acceptance.

I open my suitcase and take out my nightgown. I don't feel like hanging my clothes in the closet yet. I take the paperwork out of my backpack: the evaluation forms I'll have to fill out as I meet the teachers, administrators, and other staff members; the checklist of important points to consider; the model contract for affiliated schools that they'll have to sign, assuming they pass the evaluation. Months back, before I'd even agreed to visit this school, they would've been sent a packet detailing the benchmarks they'd have to meet so that they could adapt their rules, programmes, and instruction to the recommended standards. During this visit, it was my job to confirm that everything was functioning properly.

I pile the Garlik Institute paperwork beside the ream of paper, turn off the computer and the printer. I pace uselessly around the bedroom a few times. I take out my contacts and put them in their case. I immediately put on my prescription glasses with their thick lenses and tortoiseshell frames since I don't yet have the lie of the land and I wouldn't want to trip over something and fall on my face; it would be a bad start to show up at Saint Peter's with unexplained bruises. I look in the mirror, even through the thick lenses I can see my blue eyes, my old eyes, the ones I no longer have. My exhaustion begins to win out, I yawn and the air feels stuffy, as if the apartment has been sealed shut for too long. I push back the curtains, open the sliding door onto the balcony. The dim light of a streetlamp falls over the iron handrail and the brick wall topped with a decorative crown moulding. I look one way and the other – now I am willing to look – and I try to remember what I'd see if my vision could penetrate the darkness of the night. The house I lived in, Mariano's parents' house, Saint Peter's School. The railway crossing. I can't make out any of those things, but I know they're out there, lying in wait. As I turn to go back into the bedroom I notice on the floor of the balcony, beside the wall, a ring of small, dark balls, almost black, elongated like sunflower seeds, scattered in an imperfect circle. I bend down but I don't touch them, they look like the droppings of some small animal. Maybe a rat has been living on the balcony. Or a pigeon. It can't be a squirrel, like the ones that scurry through the Boston parks or in our yard at the lake house: there are no squirrels in Temperley. Maybe the animal is still somewhere nearby. Tiny droppings, definitely not a cat's. I look around, up at the roof, and from side to side but I don't see anything that could explain how they got there. Whatever animal was on this balcony doesn't seem to have made a nest. I search the kitchen for a broom and dustpan; I sweep up the little balls of unknown origin and throw them away. I return to the balcony, close the door, and then, finally I lie down.

I wake up very early, with the first light of day. I can't have slept more than four or five hours. I curse myself for leaving the curtains over the balcony door open so that the sunshine now floods my eyes. Jet lag would've made it hard to sleep as much as I needed to anyway, but direct sunlight to the face did not help. I'm annoyed, I don't like to sleep fewer than eight hours. Not only is it unhealthy but it keeps me from making the most of my day. Now

I'll have bad breath and a bad mood that I won't be able to shake all morning. My grumpiness might even last all day. I decide not to give up so easily, if I try, I might be able to doze for a couple more hours. I grope for the glasses I left on the night table, and, clutching them in my hand, I get up to close the curtain.

Before I do, I look onto the balcony. My vision is blurry so I put on my glasses. I look again, my gaze fixed on the floor, this time through my thick lenses.

And now I'm sure: the droppings are back.

The barrier arm was down. She stopped, behind two other cars. The alarm bell rang out through the afternoon silence. The red lights below the railway crossing sign blinked off and on. The lowered arm, the alarm bell, and the red lights all indicated that a train was coming. But there was no train. Two, five, eight minutes and still no train in sight. In the back seat, the kids were singing a song they'd learned earlier that afternoon in school. The children had been singing for so long that she'd tuned them out and their song did not disrupt the exterior silence of the afternoon. The first car drove around the barrier and crossed the tracks. The second car moved forward and took its place. She waited, without moving into the empty space between her car and the one in front of her. She wondered whether that driver, too, was going to cross the tracks like the first one had. And as soon as she finished the thought, the car drove forward, manoeuvred around the barrier arm, and stopped. Although she couldn't see, she imagined that the driver was looking both ways to make certain no train was coming.

'I don't speak English,' is the first thing Mr Galván says to me when he arrives to pick me up, thirty minutes after calling to say he was on his way. He goes on to explain that he's very proud of the fact that his school has 'the best English in the area'. That he will continue working to make sure it's 'even better', but that unfortunately he himself only speaks Spanish. 'Something I need to work on,' he says in Spanish. I nod my head but refuse to offer any approval. If he truly thought it was important to speak a foreign language, he'd have learned one. So I don't believe him. And without any solution for how we should communicate now, he tells me not to worry, that the director of their English programme, Mrs Patrick, is fully bilingual, having lived for many years in the United States. 'Where in the United States?' I ask and Mr Galván names a city that is not Boston. This puts me at ease. I don't know Mrs Patrick in my new life. Not in the one I left behind either. When I left, Saint Peter's School was still run by the family who had founded it almost fifty years prior. The director of the school at the time was a member of that family: Mr John Maplethorpe, a seasoned educator. I ask Mr Galván about him, saying I read about the original founders in the materials they'd sent about the school's history. 'Good teacher, horrible businessman,' Galván decreed. 'The 2001 crisis hit them hard, they had to sell the school off before it went under, but there are still a few Maplethorpes on the board of directors, more an honorary title than anything else. The parents loved them and they like to know they're still involved even though they hardly do anything these days.' I remember the last conversation I had with Mr John Maplethorpe, his efforts to help me, his words of advice: 'You have to be strong.' But I'm not strong, never was. I'm not strong even with my protective shield up, now that I've armoured myself to keep the suffering out. I'm still not strong even after all those years living with Robert. Mine was a lost cause: no one can be strong when an entire community has turned against them. Mr Maplethorpe hadn't, but that wasn't enough. He was a wise man, a shaper of minds, a true educator, so different to the image of a successful businessman projected by most owners of private schools today. I always thought that Robert and Mr Maplethorpe should've met. He cared more about the educational level at Saint Peter's than the business of running it so I'm not surprised that he didn't know what to do when the 2001 financial crisis threatened to do away with the school entirely. So he found a buyer. He hadn't known what to do with me either, a few years prior, besides bringing me a box of chocolates and telling me: 'You have to be strong.' I was unable to follow his advice but I will always remember those words as the only kind gesture I received during that difficult time.

Mr Galván's appearance does not match the image that came to mind when I heard his name: he's short, bald, and overweight. But he carries himself as if he thought he were extremely sexy. He speaks as if he were sexy, moves as if he were sexy. Smiles as if he were sexy. And he reeks of a suffocating cologne that he undoubtedly believes is what a sexy man would wear. Too much time surrounded by his mostly female staff must've given him the impression that he's more attractive than he actually is. It's not that there are no men in education, but women are usually the majority at any given school. Some random male teacher every once in a while. They walk into the teachers' lounge and are surrounded by a cloud of oestrogen as thick as a swarm of mosquitoes. No testosterone in the air, or very little. At the Garlik Institute the male/female ratio is a bit more balanced. But, in my recollection, Argentine schools mostly match the proportion I see on the Saint Peter's staff list. About 85% women, 15% men. The men of Saint Peter's: two PE teachers, a sociology teacher, a chemistry teacher, a design and technology teacher, and maybe one more I'm forgetting. So Mr Galván holds a privileged position as the school principal, combined with the fact that he's one of only a few men. That abundance of attention would make any man feel sexy, unless they're oblivious, and Mr Galván does not seem oblivious.

As we're getting in the car, the building's doorman comes over to ask if everything was to my liking, if I need anything – he must've been assigned the task of being solicitous with the occupants of the apartment belonging to Saint Peter's, even when he's not asked. I'm about to say that everything's fine – compulsory question, compulsory answer – but then I remember the droppings. Mr Galván acts exaggeratedly surprised by my comment, as if he himself were to blame for them. 'What an unpleasant occurrence,' Galván says. The doorman assures me that what I'm describing is highly unusual because the building is fumigated monthly. But he admits that with so many trees nearby it could've been some small animal stopping to eat the bugs that flutter around the balcony light. He suggests that I leave the light off tonight to see if the 'occurrence' repeats itself, and he looks to Mr Galván as he borrows his euphemism. I know that the balcony light wasn't left on last night because I stepped out – searching for Mariano's parents' house, my house – and everything was dark, only dimly lit by the streetlamp. And I didn't even see where the light switch was. But I don't say any of this because I don't want to undermine the doorman's theory, it's always better to leave some possible hypothesis, if not the problem seems unsolvable and that's even more worrying than a twenty-three-second silence between two people who hardly know each other.

In addition to his advice about the light, the doorman offers to take a look at the balcony later that day, when I get back from the school. I agree and thank him, but I know I won't feel like visitors after my first day at Saint Peter's. Before starting the car, Mr Galván backs up the conversation and asks what kind of animal the doorman is thinking of when he talks about nocturnal visits in search of insects. 'Bats,' the doorman responds. Bats, I think. And immediately a childhood memory pops into my head: bats would swoop over the terrace of my apartment in Caballito from time to time. Sometimes, in the mornings, several little bats might be hanging by their feet from the screen. If the door was open or we were on the balcony and my mother saw a bat she'd go into a blind panic. 'Your hair, your hair,' she would shriek as she rushed over to pull my hair back into a kind of improvised bun and then tied up her own with the same urgency. Then she'd tell the story of a girl who got a bat tangled up in her hair and they had to cut it all off to separate it from her head. The image haunted me in my dreams. The claws of a winged rodent caught in my hair. Despite my mother's insistence that her story was true, my father didn't believe it: 'Don't scare the child with that nonsense, it's just an old wives' tale.' But she swore that the girl was the daughter of a friend of a friend – without ever giving the name of one friend or the other – which guaranteed that the events were real. Unlike my father, I accepted the story of the bat and the hair unquestioningly and even enjoyed it – beyond the terrifying thought of a bat tangled up in my hair – because it was one of the rare situations in which my mother ever seemed spirited about anything and one of the infrequent occasions she had to touch me, even if it was only to tie a ribbon in my hair.

It all happens in a flash: Mr Galván asks what animal, the doorman says *murciélago*, I think *bat* in English, the memory of the bats from my childhood in Caballito, and I automatically move my hands to my hair — not remembering that I now wear it cut like a man's, short red hair that the bat from my mother's story could never get tangled in. The whole sequence occurs in an instant. It takes so many words to recount events that occur in a matter of minutes, seconds, fractions of time that are barely perceptible. Things happen so quickly that the words needed to describe them are never able to keep up. Just as it can take years for fleeting events to be forgotten. Sometimes, those memories will never fade. An instant can stay with us our entire lives, relived in words a thousand times over like a punishment. Time is compressed and the narration of that time has to expand it to make it comprehensible.

The bat issue keeps me from paying attention to the route Mr Galván takes, which by chance — or luck as my mother would say, a little luck — doesn't pass any of my prohibited places. I still have my hand in my hair, rubbing the short bristles at the top of my neck, when I realize that we've arrived. Mr Galván stops in front of Saint Peter's School and someone comes over to take his car keys so they can park it for him. Before, twenty years back, the school didn't have its own garage, there weren't that many of us. There weren't as many cars on the streets of Temperley either. Maybe some father on his way to work hurriedly dropping off his kids and rushing away. Not all families had a car available for the mother to drive the kids to school — I did have a car, back then. But back then it was more common for kids to walk to school. 'These days,' says Mr Galván, 'the older kids even come in their own cars, we don't have enough space to park them all.'

The building is just as I remembered it. A sombre, detached mansion house, white brick with dark green trim. Only they've added two more structures beside it, trying to respect the original style without much success. The sign with the school's name has changed as well. At least I think so, it's hard to remember exactly, but I don't recognize the one in front of me. I'm almost certain that the lettering is more modern now, the blue a little brighter, and under the name – Saint Peter's – they've added 'Bilingual IB since 1998'. Most likely, if they pass the tests I have to give them over the next week, they'll change the sign again so they can say: 'Garlik Licensed, Certified Affiliated School'. And they'll add the corresponding shield, our shield.

The first day is for touring the facilities, paperwork, administrative duties. The evaluations will come later. Each teacher will be evaluated individually and the administrative staff will be scored as a whole. The individual interviews are the most important aspect of the evaluation. They start out with a bit of informal, introductory conversation, to get to know the teacher before they feel like they're being evaluated even though they already are. Then the questions begin. The first series aims to assess the teacher's technical knowledge of the material as well as their teaching methods. The second series digs deeper into issues of personality and attitudes towards teaching. Finally, each teacher completes a writing exercise on a topic of their choice – if it has nothing to do with the subject they teach, all the better. Their text shows us not only their use of language, but whether they chose to write about themselves, others, in past or present tense, a true story or a piece of fiction. First, second, or third person. The evaluation is exhaustive and the great weight placed on each teacher's preparation is also the method's Achilles heel, where the few criticisms have focused: high rates of teacher turnover can mean that staff changes every year, even within a single school year. Robert defended it by saying that 'No school with high teacher turnover can be that good: if educators are well-paid, motivated, given responsibilities in line with their interest and commitment, the staff will stay relatively stable.' He even included this in the handbook we send out to each school that applies to become an 'affiliated institution' under the Garlik Certificate. Argentina is a particular place and Robert never fully understood when I told him about informal working practices, unpaid overtime, additional training being something that depended on each teacher's own initiative, all exams, essays, and projects corrected by the teacher at home in their own time, in hours they're not paid for, as they make dinner and care for their own kids. Robert said I was exaggerating, that it couldn't be as bad as I claimed, that my traumas surrounding Argentina kept me from seeing it objectively. I always ended up agreeing that I probably saw things as worse than they were. But I said it just to end the pointless discussion, not because I believed he was right. I understood that Robert couldn't understand. And I was more accepting of the reality that I knew so well, the context that was familiar to me even if it had been so many years since I'd lived there. Here, that is.

I follow Mr Galván down halls I instantly recognize but which until today had been locked out of reach, huddled at the edges of my memory. I'm constantly aware that I could run into someone I knew at any moment. It's inevitable. There must be someone from back then still here. The abyss both attracts and repels.

I try to remain calm. I tell myself that I'm protected by my new eye colour, my red hair so short it will not be of interest to any bat, my accent and my raspy voice when I speak Spanish with Mr Galván because he doesn't speak any other language, the twenty pounds I've lost. And my name: Mary Lohan. I pass classrooms I've been inside of, windows I've looked out of, I cross the school yard that looks exactly like I remembered it: the flagpole in the centre, a paved court and then grass, a few trees, the same trees, I imagine. Galván talks and I hardly listen. I once again question whether it was a good idea to have come. I have the sinking sensation that everything is going to go horribly wrong, that I won't be able to evaluate Saint Peter's due to my own incompetence and that my trip will end in disaster. That I'll return to Boston without having completed the task assigned to me and they'll fire me from the Garlik Institute – being Robert Lohan's widow won't matter if I make a huge mess of the job I was given. But I remember Robert and I take heart. The fact that he was willing to send me here means I can do it.

I'm now thinking only of him – not Robert, but him – I can't help it, I can feel him here, walking beside me. I tell him to go away but he comes back, tugs at my hand, hides on the other side of Mr Galván. I know he can't still be here twenty years later, but there he is, following me wherever I go, looking exactly the same as he did back then, as if he weren't – like me – twenty years older. Years that would've erased the softness of his skin, that might have dulled the brightness of his eyes as they did mine, that made his steps surer, more adult, but also more sombre and preoccupied. Speculation, pure speculation. I don't know what he's like today. I don't know where he is today. Whether he's still in Temperley, or even in Argentina. I don't even know if he's alive. What if he's not alive? No, that's not possible.

The day ends and Mr Galván drives me back to the apartment. Instead of feeling relief that this first day has gone smoothly, I'm unsettled by the fact that I didn't run into anyone I know or who knows me. It's true that the interviews haven't started yet, but I saw the entire school, walked every hall, worked in the office they assigned me, went out to buy painkillers for a headache, sat with Mrs Patrick drinking coffee on the couch in the front office, and I didn't see a single face I recognized. I check the staff list again towards the end of the afternoon and only vaguely recognize three names. Susana Triglia, Dolores Almada, and Verónica López, I think about those names as I look out the window of Mr Galván's car and let him tell me a story I'm not paying attention to about a trip he once took to Washington, 'but I've never been to Boston'. I think they might be people I knew back then, but I can't put faces to the names. Or even remember what they did, or if they were friends of mine or acquaintances or what. Their names are just familiar sounds, like a song I vaguely recognize having heard before. I can't link that music to any concrete memory. I've erased so much of those years. In an effort to forget what caused me so much pain, I forgot the everyday yet inoffensive details as well, street names, businesses, friends, relatives. But it didn't do any good. Even though I've stripped myself of so many memories, the pain is still there, starker and more brutal on its empty stage with all the spotlights focused on it. Everything I saw today was foreign to me: young people who couldn't possibly have been teachers back in the days I was in and out of that school. High turnover, something Robert subtracted points for, a first strike against Saint Peter's. I wonder how long I can keep going on like this, without running into anyone I know, without anyone discovering me. Maybe I didn't see anyone I know or who knows me even by name because that encounter wasn't meant for today, it's reserved for a later date. The calm before the storm. Maybe today was the calm and the interviews will be the storm, brewing on the horizon, about to soak me to the bone.

I enter the apartment building and walk over to the doorman, who seems to have been waiting for me. He asks me to please check if there is any poo on the balcony again. I'm surprised to hear him say 'poo' after having spoken of an 'occurrence' before. As if because Mr Galván is no longer present, he feels permitted to call things by their names. Or as if he's trying to be friendlier with me, warmer. I tell him that I'll check and let him know, but I'm not going to. Once I get inside the apartment I'll lock the door behind me and I won't open it again until tomorrow morning. I can't handle talking to anyone else today.

I set my things on the desk and go into the bedroom, I open the door to the balcony: fresh droppings. It's a really strange place for them, right up against the outside wall. There's nothing a bat could hang from above the circle of droppings: no light, no beam, no brace. I look up and check again to make sure. I wonder why I never saw bat droppings on the balcony of my parents' house even though they visited our terrace regularly. I imagine my father hurriedly cleaning them up or shaking one of his books at them, the pages acting as an improvised broom sweeping the little black balls to the street below before my mother saw them and rushed to tie my hair up.

I go into the bedroom, rummage in my purse, and step back onto the balcony with a lit cigarette – I haven't been a regular smoker for years, it's not good for my dysphonia, but I always carry a pack with me and today I need one. Not in my mouth so much as in my hand, to roll it against my index and middle fingers, my thumb, hold it in the air and watch it burn, the thread of smoke snaking around my head. I sit on the floor and wait. I don't know what I'm waiting for, but I wait. No animal appears. I take a drag, let the ash fall into the bowl I create with my left hand. I stand up and look for the switch to turn on the balcony light. I go back outside, look up again, sit leaning against the wall opposite the one where the droppings keep appearing. I wait. After a little while the light becomes crowded with insects: mosquitoes, moths, bugs I don't know the names of in Spanish or in English. I feel hopeful. But no bat appears. I touch my hair as if I still had hair that a bat could get tangled in, as if my mother could still today tie it up in a bun. I take three or four more drags from my cigarette. I think about how it takes so many words to describe a single instant and how an instant can last a lifetime no matter what words are used to explain it away. This bat who comes to leave its droppings on my balcony must know everything an instant can contain: flapping blindly under that light, hunting all the insects it can then disappearing.

I stub out the half-burnt cigarette, I set it aside. I close my eyes, doze off for a little while, I'm not sure how long. Maybe minutes, half an hour, who knows, I cannot be certain of anything as the moments slip away.

The only thing certain is that when I open my eyes there are fresh droppings of unknown origin.

I'm dreading the weekend. It's still days away but Mr Galván is already threatening to show me around, organize an asado, introduce me to some friends. I reject all of his offers politely but firmly. I tell him that I have to work, I'm writing something and I need a weekend alone to edit the latest draft. I'm not lying, in actual truth I'm writing this text – this 'logbook' that I started at Kennedy airport, after travelling by train from Boston to New York. The week ahead, however, with its set routine, no longer intimidates me. I'll spend all day at the school evaluating each and every one of the teachers – the interview changes but it's pretty much the same scene repeated over and over. Then I'll return to the apartment where the doorman will greet me with some new hypothesis about the droppings on the balcony, and not much else. Maybe a brief walk through the neighbourhood every once in a while, each time a little further, but without ever going near the places that are off limits. Is he still where I left him? I want to see him but I don't want to see him at the same time, in the same wish. I'm more inclined towards the first option out of cowardice, to keep from opening myself up to risk. But what's worse? Having to face him, to look him in the eye? Or being this close and not contacting him, not seeking him out, not at least trying to see him even if only this one last time. I think Robert wanted me to come so that I could finally ask myself these questions. Questions I didn't allow myself to ask for years. Just being able to ask the question is more important than the answer I don't yet have. All I know is that I can't even imagine what it would be like to see his eyes, twenty years older, staring into mine. What would I say to him? What would he say to me? I don't have the answer but I will wait for it to come. Not silently, like I did all those years, now I can at least pose the question. And I try to focus on my assigned task, try to complete the evaluation efficiently, on time, so I can return safe and sound to Boston, my home. This other place – Temperley – where I lived – is still foreign to me. It will always be foreign to me.

I asked Mr Galván not to pick me up so I could walk to school this morning. But I choose the route I traced on Google Maps before the plane took off, the route that won't take me past any prohibited places. I hardly recognize the streets, the shops. Some of the houses I can't find must have been replaced by apartment buildings. Old shops have disappeared and new ones have taken their places. I'm disoriented by the different colours, the different architecture – the new houses don't match that English-style neighbourhood I remember, now it's all a jumble of buildings plastered with political campaign ads for people I know nothing about, litter along the sides of the streets, no empty lots left at all. There's more traffic, more noise, more people coming and going. I'm surprised to find that being here – even though it has all changed so much – hasn't brought the past flooding back. Even despite the efforts I made for so long to forget it. I know I'm anaesthetized, muted, but it still surprises me. I go into a shop, then another, constantly on the lookout for some shopkeeper that I knew from years ago, when I was blonde, when I had blue eyes. Until I realize that I'm not searching for someone I recognize as much as someone who recognizes me. In spite of my red hair, my thinness, my brown eyes. But this time it's not the abyss pulling me in, it's not the sense of danger, the imminent risk of the trick being revealed. It's something else: I did everything I could to forget them, I killed them inside my mind, but did they kill me too? Does no one see me? Did anyone ever see me? If I hadn't been there that day at the railway crossing, would anyone have seen me? Finally, at the drugstore the pharmacist pauses as she's handing me my change for the aspirin I'm buying. She holds the bills in the air without giving them to me. She looks me in the eye: 'You remind me of someone,' she says. My legs go weak. I can't speak, I wait. I'm scared but also relieved that someone has recognized me, despite the weight loss, the red hair. 'But no,' she says, 'no offence, but if you knew who you remind me of...' 'Who?' I mumble, barely more than a whisper. I ask again without raising my voice: 'Who?' She won't say who, just: 'Best to forget about her. A horrible woman, never mind, I'm sorry...' She hands me the change and looks to the next customer. I can't seem to move from where I'm standing with my aspirin and the change in my hand. I remain fixed to that spot in front of her. 'Sorry,' she says again, 'never mind.' She apologizes for an offense that I'm not supposed to understand, but I do understand. I walk outside, take a few steps, and I start to cry. Finally, I cry. My contacts go cloudy. Everything blurs. A horrible woman.

My eyes are still moist when I reach Saint Peter's. I go directly to the bathroom. Whenever I cry my contacts shift and I see everything blurry. My eye doctor says it doesn't happen to everyone who wears contacts, only people who cry 'a specific way'. I search in my purse for my contact solution but I didn't bring it with me. Tap water won't work. I have to use my own saliva, the liquid most similar to the contact solution I don't have. I leave the bathroom somewhat more composed, I go to my office and turn on the computer. Mr Galván pokes his head in and informs me that the list of teachers to be interviewed has undergone some minor modifications due to changes in staff – that turnover Robert would subtract points for – and he acts surprised that I never received the email detailing the changes. I suspect that Mr Galván never sent the email, that the teachers were only recently replaced by new ones. So he makes up an excuse about the message getting lost in cyberspace. He tells me he'll resend it right away but doesn't. I don't care one way or another, knowing the names of the interviewees ahead of time won't make any difference. Or so I think.

The interviews up to now have all been fairly similar and I have to admit that the teachers I've evaluated seem adequately trained for the tasks assigned to them. Susan Triglia, who I interview on the second day, did turn out to be someone I knew – just as I suspected. A teacher who'd joined the school a year or two before the event that forced me to leave. I didn't know her, but I remember her face from the audience at school plays, sporting events, and end of year celebrations. I don't think she remembers me. Or at least she wouldn't remember me if I hadn't become some sad celebrity in that educational community. Anyway, I'm certain that I never interacted with her much, so by mid-morning – and given Triglia's poor memory, made evident in the interview – I take comfort that she'll never figure out who I really am.

Verónica López is on the list of teachers but she's no longer employed at the school and as I was waiting for her the door opened and a young man in his twenties walked in. It turned out to be the teacher who had recently replaced her – one of the staff changes Galván claimed to have informed me of in the email he never sent.

But when Dolores Almada's turn comes my stomach does a flip. I did know her, well. I wouldn't say we were friends – I now know that I never had friends here – but we definitely had considerable interaction with each other. I hadn't been able to place her before when I looked at the list, even though her name had sounded an alarm bell. I'd known her by her married name, Valenti. Back then, she didn't work at the school or anywhere, she spent all her time running around after her twin boys who were always misbehaving. And she used her married name. She shakes my hand and introduces herself now – 'Dolores Almada, pleased to meet you' – she informs me that she has a degree in biochemistry – how did I never know that? – and that she works at the school as a Science teacher. I immediately put my guard up, but as she continues to drone on like she's never seen me before in her life, my fear turns to irritation. This woman has been to my house, she's shared meals with me, birthday parties, how is it possible she doesn't recognize me? During the second battery of questions I stare her down, willing her to detect my true identity. But Dolores Almada is so worried about her evaluation, about making a good impression on this person, Mary Lohan, that it never occurs to her I could be someone else. She becomes anxious, thinking my expression indicates that her answers are unsatisfactory. So she makes an exaggerated effort to appear confident, providing longwinded explanations. Whereas all I want is for her to falter. During the second set of questions her failure to recognize me is so infuriating that I want to shout in her face: 'Don't you know who I am?' Right before the interview ends I really think I might do it. But I stop myself, I wrap up the questions, ask her to find a comfortable spot to write her personal essay and bring it to me in an hour. Without waiting for her to get up, I excuse myself and go to the bathroom. I splash water on my face. I look at myself in the mirror, I start crying again, this time not because my feelings are hurt like they were by the pharmacist's comment but because maybe there's truly nothing of the old me left.

An hour later, Dolores Almada hands in her personal essay and I read it as soon as she leaves. A throwaway text, filled with clichés, unnecessary adjectives – the white snow, the gentle breeze, the warm afternoon. It won't affect her evaluation negatively; Dolores Almada's mediocre, impersonal, horrible text gives me a certain satisfaction. But the use of the word 'horrible' applied to her text reminds me of the pharmacist's use of that same word. I cry for the third time in one day. My contact lenses shift out of place. I remove them but I don't wash them with my saliva and put them back in. I put on my glasses instead; it would be pointless to clean them, I'll probably start crying again. This time I'm crying because language – like a treacherous route you try to avoid – can be a slippery slope leading down into the places that hurt the most.

The day wears on, predictably, as I go through my scheduled interviews. But then, towards the end of the afternoon when everything seems to be under control, a little while after I put my contacts back in because I think there will be no more tears and I've almost forgotten about the pharmacist and Dolores Almada, when my anxiety has calmed and the only question in my mind is whether or not there will be more mysterious droppings on my balcony, what was bound to happen finally occurs. After so many days of conflicting feelings, unable to decide whether I want to be seen or to pass unnoticed, feeling bold enough to walk the streets of the neighbourhood but always avoiding the places that feel most threatening, wondering whether it would be more tragic to see him or to return to Boston without having seen him one last time, today, here in this very school, the door opens and there he stands, right in front of me, with one hand on the doorknob and a book in the other. My heart stops. I know that it must still be ticking, beating even faster than normal in fact. But I feel like my heart stops beating. I might not have recognized him, it's been many years, in fact I'm not fully certain it is him standing in front of me. But an alarm goes off inside my body, telling me that it's him, and then I look down at the list, searching for the name of the teacher who's supposed to be there. And it's his name on the page. It sticks into my stomach like a knife. I look back up at him. His gaze, young, innocent, free of guilt and worry, meets mine. His voice, a different voice, asks if I'm Mary Lohan. And I can't respond. I try to stand but I'm unable to do so or to make even the slightest gesture indicating that yes, that I'm Mary Lohan for him too. Because there, in front of me, somewhere I never dreamed of seeing him – but why not here? – there he is, the person who despite my lack of response takes two or three steps towards me and informs me that he's the high school history teacher, that we have a meeting first thing tomorrow morning and he wanted to make sure I had his name down on the list and not the name of the teacher he replaced a month back, Mrs Marta Galíndez. Him. After the initial shock, the vertigo, I'm now certain. It's still him, even though over twenty years have passed. And I verify that my heart did not in fact stop because it's now pounding so loudly he can probably hear it from across the room. My palms sweat. The pen I was writing with slips out of my hand and rolls across the floor. He bends down to pick it up, takes a few steps closer, and holds it out to me as he says his name, which I already know: Federico Lauría. His hand beside my hand, holding out a pen that has just fallen. A hand I once knew so well, that I still know. His eyes on mine. And then his eyes fall to my hand. The pen as a bridge between us.

Finally he looks up and says: 'See you tomorrow.'

He looks back down at my hand – now gripping the pen – and he stares at it. All the energy and enthusiasm he entered my office with seconds ago seems to have suddenly drained from his body. He stands there frozen in silence for an instant that I can't calculate in seconds, or in words.

I would've liked to stay there like that, him and I both motionless, silent. But after a moment he gently shakes his head, as if waking from a trance or returning from a daydream that took him somewhere far away.

He says goodbye and leaves.

My son leaves.

The barrier arm was down. She stopped, behind two other cars. The alarm bell rang out through the afternoon silence. The red lights below the railway crossing sign blinked off and on. The lowered arm, the alarm bell, and the red lights all indicated that a train was coming. But there was no train. Two, five, eight minutes and still no train in sight. In the back seat, the kids were singing a song they'd learned earlier that afternoon in school. 'Incy Wincy spider went up the water spout.' The children had been singing for so long that she'd tuned them out and their song did not disrupt the exterior silence of the afternoon. 'Down came the rain and washed the spider out.' The first car drove around the barrier and crossed the tracks. The second car moved forward and took its place. She waited, without moving into the empty space between her car and the one in front of her. 'Out came the sun and dried up all the rain.' She wondered whether that driver, too, was going to cross the tracks like the first one had. And as soon as she finished the thought, the car drove forward, manoeuvred around the barrier arm, and stopped. Although she couldn't see, she imagined that the driver was looking both ways to make certain no train was coming.

I don't know how I made it back to the apartment. I'm not sure if Mr Galván brought me, if I walked, if I got in a taxi. I don't know if the doorman was waiting for me when I got back to the building. Or how I managed to find the keys in my purse and fit them into the lock. It was like I opened my eyes after being in a coma and found myself here where I am: sitting on the balcony, beside the droppings, shivering, with my knees pressed to my chest, my arms hugging my legs, my hands gripping my elbows. Crying. The time between the moment my son's eyes met mine, fell to my hand, to this moment, now, on the balcony, simply vanished. There's no way to reconstruct the sequence of events, no way to recount what happened. There's only a black hole, void of words, images, smells; I've had other blank spots, between one moment and another much later one.

My son twenty years later. My son introducing himself to me at the end of the day. My son who'll come back to my office tomorrow morning so I can ask him stupid questions that will allow me to evaluate him as an educator – as a history teacher – when all I want to do is… hug him? Cry with him? Ask him to forgive me even though I know his answer might hurt as much as these years away from him have? Why did my son decide to study history, if that is in fact what he studied? What teacher, mentor, book, or event inspired that six-year-old boy to become a history teacher? Can I allow myself to imagine that it was something I sowed in him during the few years we lived together? How much of Federico – who a few hours ago opened the door of my office and introduced himself – was already there, inside that boy I left behind? What role did my absence have in the shaping of the man he is today? A black hole. The years he lived without me, the years I lived without him. I don't know what I'm supposed to do now, face to face with my son, twenty years later, I never allowed myself to imagine it. Never allowed myself to feel it. And I certainly never imagined it would be an interview about how he plans, structures, and administers his history lessons to the students of Saint Peter's School.

I cry, inconsolably, hugging my legs. I cry out my contact lenses, gripping my tortoiseshell glasses in case I need to put them on to see something. But I don't need to see, just to cry. I cry loudly, my body making movements that look like convulsions. I'm hyperventilating. And then I stop, take a deep breath, try to control my breathing and return to a state of calm that seems impossible to achieve. But just when I think I'm back in control, I start crying again. Hours pass. I can tell because the light on the balcony changes, imperceptibly at first, then more obviously, until little by little lights and shadows establish a new equilibrium. The afternoon light fades into deep night, and later the dawn once again restores contours, treetops, a sign that flickers due to some electrical glitch. I don't know if I slept at all. Or if I sat here awake. My eyes sting so badly I don't think I can put my contacts in. If I somehow manage to scrape myself off this floor and face the day ahead of me, I'll wear the ugly, thick glasses that will put more distance between me and my son. I rub my eyes, they sting as if my corneas were lined with splinters stabbing into my brain. And I realize that, despite the pain, I'll have to put in my contacts, because I'm now Mary Lohan, not Marilé, and I don't have blue eyes any more. I have to put in those contacts because I have to face my son with brown eyes, with eyes that he's never seen. I unfold my arms from around my legs and run my hands over my chest, my shoulders, up and down my arms in an attempt to warm myself. I know I have to pull myself up off this cold balcony that digs into my tailbone. That I have to take a shower. Get dressed. Put in my contacts. Pick up my folders, my purse, act like nothing happened at Saint Peter's. But I don't know if I can. As soon as I try, I might fall right back down onto this floor, and nothing will be able to get me up.

The doorbell rings. I don't answer it. It rings again. Whoever's there is so insistent that I finally gather the energy to stand, put on my glasses, and walk to the door to see who it is. I open it a crack without removing the chain, it's the doorman. He cheerfully informs me that he has good news. I remove the chain and open the door a little wider, but I don't invite him in. He stares at my glasses but doesn't say anything. Then he smiles widely and starts speaking quickly, moving his hands, gesticulating, pointing to the balcony, probably telling me that he's solved the mystery of the droppings but I only deduce this because I'm not listening; I can hear his voice but I don't understand the words he's saying. I want to cry but I can't because there's a man in front of me talking non-stop about the droppings on the balcony where I spent all night shivering with cold thinking about my son. I finally catch one word: poo. He says 'poo' and then 'mess', but I transform his words into 'droppings', as if it were a translation of a novel written in some other language. Droppings. Until at some point the doorman looks at me and something in my eyes, even through the thick lenses, makes him stop. He stares at me but doesn't have the nerve to ask if there's something wrong. I take off my glasses and I look at him. 'I had a problem with my contacts and my eyes are irritated.' The doorman seems relieved. I don't know if he believes me, but he's relieved anyway. 'They're blue,' he says. 'What are?' I ask. 'Your eyes, sorry, from so much... Sorry, your eyes have turned blue.' Embarrassed, he tries to escape his own words. He walks into the apartment without asking for permission and goes directly to the balcony. He points to the moulding above our heads, 'You know what that is right there?' he says and he smiles. 'Wood,' I say. 'Behind the wood, ma'am,' he laughs as if he's told a joke. 'I don't know what's behind it.' 'A little bat's made a nest in there. I suspected it and then yesterday when I tapped the wood it squealed like a rat, the little devil. Easy to fix, ma'am, I'll pour some poison in, seal it off at the top and bottom, and in a couple of days it'll be dead. It'll be trapped in there until it dies.' Trapped to death, unable to get out. I hear the sound of an alarm bell and a train approaching. I cry. I can cry now, even with this man standing here in front of me. I cover my face with my hands. I clumsily wipe at my tears, only spreading the dampness around my face. The doorman is unsettled, he knows what to do about a bat who's made a nest on the balcony but not about a crying woman. He reaches out to place a hand on my shoulder but stops himself. 'Don't worry, I'll take care of it,' he says in an attempt to calm me. 'It's not that,' I say, but he doesn't hear me. 'You're scared, all women are scared of bats,' he tells me and I don't say anything because I don't care about women and their fears, only about this little bat who has just learned to fly and who's now going to be trapped in there, unable to get out, awaiting its death sentence. 'I can bring the poison and the caulk up right now and we'll solve the problem straight away. It'll dry right up like a leaf, I promise,' he says. And I repeat his words: 'It's going to be trapped in there, it won't be able to get out, dry as a leaf.' I start crying again. The doorman is made even more nervous by the fact that the solution he offered to soothe me has had the opposite effect. He looks down to the street to avoid looking at me, unsure whether he should say something, leave, or wait for me to collect myself. I know the man wants to go, to run away, to escape my emotions. 'No, not again,' I say firmly, but he doesn't understand. How could the doorman possibly understand. Did my son understand? I reach up to the wooden moulding, I knock on it like the man says he knocked the day before. The animal squeals. 'See,' he says, 'there it is.' I spin around to face him, furious: 'I won't allow it.' The doorman is even more confused, this situation doesn't fit into his universe of possibilities. 'It's a bat,' he says. 'I don't want you to leave it trapped in there,' I say. And then I shout: 'I won't let it die trapped in there!' The doorman is alarmed, and, like a child who's been scolded, says: 'Okay, okay, fine, whatever you want, I don't care about the bat shit, it's on your balcony, not mine. Sorry... excuse my language,' he adds, as if 'poo' had been pushing the limits but 'shit' was a word of another order, something you had to apologize for. We stood there, both of us silent, for what felt like an eternity. Much longer than the awkward twenty-three-second silence Robert talked about. Finally the man says: 'Or I could smoke it out then seal the hole up and it'll find another place to make a nest. Would that be all right with you?' I tell him I'm not sure, to let me think about it. I feel like crying again but I clench my throat closed and hold it in. 'Well, just let me know,' he says and he takes that moment of tentative resolution as his chance to escape. 'I'll let you know,' I say.

The doorman leaves, I stand on the balcony staring at the wooden moulding, thinking about the little bat and the decision I have to make as to where it will live or if it will live at all. To decide once again who lives and who dies. I try to picture the bat, I don't know exactly what a baby bat looks like but I imagine it's warm. I run my hand over the wood. I lean against the wall, not caring that I'm stepping in its droppings. Its mess. I rest my hand on the wood, as if in doing so I might be able to feel the animal trapped inside. I think about my son. And about that other boy named Juan. And about myself. The three of us all trapped in different ways.

I'm still trapped. I must now decide whether to go out and face the task at hand or stay here and wait for the poison to kill me or the smoke to force me out.

I get in the shower and as the hot water washes over my body I prepare myself to face Federico, my son. I imagine myself saying his name, watching him as he sits across from me, making up questions that aren't on Robert's list so that I can find out who he lives with, who took care of him all those years, who put him to bed, who talked to him about love, death, infinity, pain. Find out if he's happy. If he was able to be happy. I make up questions that I know I won't ask. I go over them again and again, edit them, discard a few, add a few others. I memorize them. Until I finally get dressed, put in my contacts, gather my things, and go downstairs. This bat has chosen to come out from behind the wood and face the light.

Mr Galván is waiting outside. We must've agreed on this yesterday but his words were sucked into that black hole that opened up between my son's eyes and the balcony where a bat made its nest.

Before I leave, the doorman asks if I've decided what I want to do. I don't know what he's referring to.

'About the bat,' he says.

'The bat already flew away,' I answer.

I'm sitting behind the desk in the office Saint Peter's has lent me to complete my work. I'm waiting for the history teacher, Federico Lauría. Waiting for my son. I check my watch, it's five minutes past the hour he was supposed to be here. I'm surprised he's late. My entire body trembles imperceptibly. I have the evaluation forms and a pen laid out on the desk. But I don't know if I'll be able to use them, I don't know if I'll be able to write, I don't know if I'll be able to utter a single word. Ten minutes after the scheduled time my son has yet to arrive. What if he doesn't come? What if something has happened to him? I ask myself the questions all mothers must ask when their son goes out and doesn't come back on time. Questions that I learned never to ask myself.

Fifteen minutes after the scheduled time Federico finally turns up. He opens the door without knocking and walks across the room: 'Excuse the delay,' he says and sits down in front of me. He doesn't give me a kiss on the cheek – the typical greeting in Argentina – and he doesn't even shake my hand. His impersonal attitude is appropriate for the professional relationship we have here today. It's logical but strange nonetheless to greet my son, after twenty years, without so much as touching. 'Should we get started?' he says. And I'm grateful to him for kicking things off because I could've sat there for all of eternity, just staring at him. 'Let's,' I say.

My son effortlessly answers questions about his job. He's clear and concise. But he seems tense, not like he was yesterday afternoon. Yesterday he was happy, confident, walking on air. Today he's different, or so it seems to me. Maybe something's happened, something personal, something in his family which I'm no longer a part of. Or maybe the stress of being tested has caused him to become withdrawn, as happens with some people. Other people react by going into excessive detail, talking non-stop. I ask where he went to university and I find out that my son got an undergrad degree in history from the University of Buenos Aires and that he's currently enrolled in a PhD programme. I'm sure his father disapproves of that decision – unless Mariano has changed a lot. I suspect that he tried to talk his son into getting a degree that would've allowed him to join the family business – just as Mariano had done – to carry on the legacy of everything they'd worked towards 'for generations'. He would've at the very least wanted his son to get a degree that would allow him to make some money. Mariano was always very pragmatic above all else and for him a person's success is measured – or was measured, what do I know about what Mariano thinks now – by their economic achievements. I get lost in the imaginary dialogue between Federico and his father but come back to the interview when I hear my son say that since he only has an undergrad degree in history and not his doctorate yet, he might still be lacking some of the pedagogical resources that would be useful in giving classes, but that he's certain he'll acquire them. And despite his limited classroom experience, he feels that he's been able to connect with the students. He talks to me about how he structures his lessons, about the evaluation methods he uses, about how he prioritizes classwork and participation over a single final exam that often fails to demonstrate what the student truly knows. Robert favoured ongoing evaluation over final exams as well. I like everything my son is saying, I like that he seems concerned with doing a good job as an educator. But even though he says all this sincerely – at least he seems sincere to me – there's a certain haste to his responses, as if he were trying to get the interview over with so he could move on to something else. I'm anxious to move on to the next phase of the interview as well. I want to get to the second battery of more personal questions so he'll have to talk about himself. But I have to stick to the protocol, ask all the questions, listen to all his answers. To take notes. I pick up the pen and discover that I am able to write. I look at the blue blazer my son wears, the white shirt with the top button undone – I wonder who irons his shirts. He wears a Swatch watch, sporty, cheap, very different to the kind his father would wear. His skin is tanned and his blue eyes light up his face. He meets my gaze when he speaks to me. But, between one question and the next, he stares down at my hands. He follows my hand as it holds the pen, from one side of the page to the other. I stop writing, his eyes stop. I turn back to the questions. We talk about different ways of engaging the students, the use of audio-visual material, essays.

Finally, forty-five minutes later, we reach the battery of personal questions. Robert designed this interview not to intrude into anyone's personal life – that would be frowned upon in the U.S. – but merely to get an idea of a teacher's personality and classroom management style, their patience for walking students through the learning process, how empathetic they are with others, their ability to manage difficult situations. 'What is your family makeup?' I ask. And I know that it's not about simply asking if the teacher is married or single, if they live alone or with their parents, but to draw conclusions about whether this person is content with their life, whatever life they've chosen. There's nothing more damaging to a student, Robert said, than a bitter teacher, a teacher who does their job grudgingly, believing they were meant for something better, that life has big things in store for them but in the meantime they have no choice but to teach. And Federico answers: 'I live with my wife and my daughter,' and I forget about Robert and his theories as I try to keep my eyes from filling with tears. My son has a daughter, I have a granddaughter. He only told me because I'm Mary Lohan and I'm evaluating him: Marilé has a granddaughter but no one would bother to let her know. 'What's her name?' I blubber, my voice trembling, even though the question is not on Robert's list. 'Amelia,' he answers, 'my wife picked it out.' And as I nod my head more times than necessary and I make a note that Robert's questionnaire does not ask me to, I'm internally processing the fact that Federico, the son I left at age six, now has a wife and a daughter. 'Amelia has blue eyes,' he says, 'it runs in the family.' And I would like to ask him to show me a picture, to let me see her face, her smile, to talk to me about her. But instead I say: 'What role does teaching play within the structure of your family?' I set aside my granddaughter's blue eyes and return to the questionnaire. 'It's my job,' he answers as if it were very obvious. 'But do you like the job or are you at all conflicted about it?' 'I love history, it's my passion, understanding why things happened, the causes and also the consequences. But the causes especially. Teaching history allows me to talk about things that interest me. Much better than the isolated life of the historian who only does research. And I'm interested in transmitting information, in teaching others what I know; if I can get someone else passionate about it, all the better. I like giving classes, also, I need to, going back to what I said before, it's my job.' 'And what does your wife do?' I ask and I cover the question form so that my son can't tell that this one isn't on the list, I just added it because I want to know about the woman he loves, assuming he loves her. I hope he does. 'She's finishing a degree in literature, she hasn't graduated yet and now with the baby it's going to take her a little longer. She loves spending time with our daughter, she won't let anyone else take care of her,' he says, and he looks at me for a moment. Then he starts up again: 'But she's going to finish, I'm going to help her so she can finish.' Do you love her, son? Are you in love with her? I'd like to ask, but I don't, I can't, I don't have the right. Does she love you? Does she make you happy? I'd like to say, but instead I say: 'Can you tell me about your earliest educational experiences?' He looks up from my hands and stares directly into my eyes, rubs his own, takes a deep breath, pauses for a second, looking at me, and only after a tense silence asks: 'Don't you know?' I'm frozen by his response, I try to say something but I can't. My son clarifies: 'It doesn't figure in my report that I went to school here at Saint Peter's?' 'Oh, yes, yes, it does say that. I'm asking how it was for you?' I try to respond naturally but it's obvious that his comment took me by surprise. 'Difficult,' he says. And he continues: 'Up to age six everything was fine, then it got hard.' My son sits waiting for the next question, but all I can do is look at him and try to hold back the tears I feel rising up my throat. I don't want him to see me cry, I don't want my contacts to slip out of place and make everything blurry again, I don't want this interview to end in disaster. 'My parents separated and it was hard for me to get used to certain things,' my son continues. He doesn't say, 'my mother abandoned me', he says, 'my parents separated'. And that surprises me but I try not to let it get my hopes up. It can't be easy for him to tell a stranger that his mother abandoned him, that she left one day and never came back. Son, my son, I'd like to say to him, I'm sorry. I'd like to shout it. Just thinking the word 'sorry' causes my throat to close, cuts off my breathing. I try to get it out of my head. 'For example?' I manage to ask. 'Can you give me an example of something it was hard for you to get used to?' 'Living with my father and his new wife wasn't easy. She had two kids, one was a classmate of mine at school, we'd been friends before he became my "brother" but then everything changed. Even though they moved into my house, I was the one who was left out.' Who is it, son? Tell me the name of that woman who didn't know how to help you in my absence. A mother from school? Who? I can't ask, but he continues. 'I don't hold it against them, the boys or Martha.' Martha? So Mariano finally closed the loop that had opened up that summer in Pinamar. He got back together with Martha. 'She was one of my mother's friends.' My son mentions me for the first time, but he's mistaken: Martha was no friend of mine. 'I don't blame anyone, or maybe just my father for not making space for me in that new family he built. But, well, it's fine now. I have my own family. It's fine.' He only mentions me to describe his father's new wife, he says, 'a friend of my mother's', but he doesn't go into detail about his mother, he doesn't say if she died, if she left, if she stayed close by but he just didn't live with her. He says what he blames his father for but he doesn't talk about what he blames his mother for. He must blame me, a lot. But he doesn't say it. I don't know how much he knows about that day, about what happened afterward. He doesn't mention it. He doesn't talk about his mother. He doesn't talk about me. As if it were unnecessary to clarify what happened to her. As if that boy, Federico, had never had a mother beyond a noun used to modify another noun: a friend of his mother. I'd like to ask him: And what about your mother? Did you forget about her? Do you hate her? Did you kill her in your mind? But I don't say anything, and he changes the subject.

'You know, I think I wanted to study history because of my own past. In world history, or national history, there's always a reason. One event causes another and that causes another one. A domino effect. I think of history as a chain of events linked by cause and effect. Some people would say that's an oversimplification. But I think that's what the world is. Our lives too. Of course our lives aren't part of history, yet.' My son's eyes wander to the office's only window, which looks onto the school yard where the younger kids have come out to play. I let him waver there for a moment, taking the opportunity to study him, his skin no longer firm and childlike, the stubble of beard he must shave every morning, his almost perfectly straight nose, three little freckles like steps leading from his cheekbone to his right ear. My observation is cut short as he suddenly returns to the conversation. 'Getting back to the point, history,' he says, 'because of one event, that leads to another, we end up with war, the Industrial Revolution, genocide, a peace treaty, or the misnamed "discovery of America". I was never interested in the events so much as the reasons. And history always has a reason. Life, on the other hand, doesn't. You know what I mean?' he says, looking at me, waiting for an answer, his gaze demanding a response. I don't know if I do know what he means, I can hardly think, hardly breathe sitting there a few feet from him, watching him, so I don't respond but I write something down as if I knew what he meant. 'You know what I mean?' he says again. And I look up and I lie, say that yes, that I think I do know. 'I want you to know, to finally understand that some people are missing reasons in their own lives,' he says and he pulls an envelope out of his pocket and places it on the desk.

'We're done now, aren't we?' he asks. And I say: 'Yes, almost, all that's left is…' But he doesn't let me finish the sentence. 'Here's my personal essay,' he says, and he slides the envelope across the desk. 'Oh, no, sorry…' I say. 'The freewriting exercise has to be completed here, at the end of the interview, bringing it written ahead of time isn't an option.' 'This is my text, it's the only one I have in me. I'd write the exact same thing if you gave me a piece of paper and I sat down to write it. I have it memorized. I wouldn't change a word, not a single comma…' 'But…' I start to say. He keeps talking: 'It's a text I've been writing for years. I've written it a thousand times, I don't know how many. Always the same. I add details, sounds, some smell I hadn't remembered before. But it's always the same text. Always.' I try to explain that that's not the way it works: 'The idea is that you write a personal essay as part of the evaluation, it doesn't matter what…' 'Yes, it does matter, and this is it. Take it or leave it, there's no other text, there won't be any other,' my son says and he stands up. Despite my refusal to accept the text, it's clear that Federico has decided the interview is over. 'Goodbye,' he says and he turns around and leaves the room.

The door closes behind him and I sit there shaking like I shook last night on the balcony, under the bat's nest inside the moulding. I take the envelope but I don't dare open it, I still have it in my hand when my son opens the door again and says: 'The freckle.' And before he closes the door, he adds: 'I couldn't sleep last night thinking about that freckle.' And he seems like he might be about to say something else but he stops himself. Instead he clenches his fists, his face turns red, the veins on his neck, forehead, and beside his ears stand out, as if he were about to explode, he moves his lips to speak, to scream. But, then, making an obvious effort, he contains himself and says calmly: 'Everything I have to say is in there,' pointing to the envelope in my hands.

And then my son leaves, for good. I let him leave without trying to stop him. My son walks quickly and decidedly through the door that slams shut behind him, and this time he doesn't come back. And from the envelope I'm holding in my right hand, I shift my gaze to the large freckle beside the bump of my wrist bone, a pea-sized brown spot that has been with me since birth, shaped like an apple. The envelope trembles in the air. My freckle trembles with it. That freckle we played games with so many times. He would pretend that I wasn't his mama, that an alien had swapped me for someone else, I would roll down my sleeve to hide the freckle. He would chase me around the house until he caught me, push up my sleeve and say: 'The alien gave you back, you're my mama again, only my mama has that brown spot right by this bone.' He would touch the freckle and say again: 'You're my mama.'

I'm his mama.

I try to steady my shaking hands, I run a finger up my wrist until I get to that freckle. I pass the tip of my index finger over it from side to side, barely grazing it, still unsure of what to do.

PERSONAL ESSAY
by Federico Lauría

The barrier arm was down. She stopped. My mother stopped. Behind two other cars. The alarm bell rang out through the afternoon silence. I wasn't paying attention at the time, that day, but I can hear it now, always. The red lights below the railway crossing sign blinked off and on. The lowered arm, the alarm bell, and the red lights all indicated that a train was coming. A train must be coming. But there was no train. Two, five, eight minutes and still no train in sight. In the back seat, we were singing a song we'd learned earlier that afternoon in school. Juan – my classmate – and I sang. 'Incy Wincy spider went up the water spout.' We had been singing for so long that she – my mother – had tuned us out and our song did not disrupt the exterior silence of the afternoon. 'Down came the rain and washed the spider out.' The first car drove around the barrier and crossed the tracks. The second car moved forward and took its place. She waited, without moving into the empty space between her car and the one in front of her. 'Out came the sun and dried up all the rain.' She wondered whether that driver, too, was going to cross the tracks like the first one had – 'What's this guy doing, is he going to go?' And as soon as she finished the thought, the car drove forward, manoeuvred around the barrier arm, and stopped. Although she couldn't see, she imagined that the driver was looking both ways to make certain no train was coming – or so I suppose.

Finally, the only car in front of us moved forward and drove around the lowered arm. My mother hesitated. She was worried we'd be late to the movie. She had promised to take me as a treat for winning the art contest at school. 'And Incy Wincy spider climbed up the spout again.' The alarm bell kept ringing, the light kept blinking. Now I was paying attention, Juan wasn't, he kept singing. My mother turned her head to look at us. 'Why aren't we going, Mama?' I asked. 'Aren't we going to the movies?' 'I'm waiting for the train to pass,' she answered. 'What train?' I said. And she replied: 'You're right. What train am I waiting for? This crossing never works.' So my mother manoeuvred her car around the barrier arm, looked both ways, and drove forward. But as soon as she'd passed the first set of tracks, the car stalled. The engine hiccupped and stopped dead. My mother turned the key several times, but it wouldn't start. I couldn't hear the alarm bell any more – even though it was still dinging – over the coughing of the engine. Despite the many times she tried, it would not start. My mother took a deep breath. She looked at us in the rear-view mirror. She was pale, her blue eyes wide. Juan laughed. I didn't, I knew that my mother never went white like that and never opened her eyes so wide. She tried to start the car one more time but it would not obey her commands. That was when we heard the train whistle. A long, loud whistle. My mother's back stiffened, her shoulders tensed, her left fist gripped the steering wheel as she moved her right hand to turn the key several more times, desperately. Juan was still laughing, excitedly kicking the empty passenger seat in front of him, as if it were some game. I might've thought the same thing, that it was all a game, if it hadn't been for the fact that my mother was sitting in the front seat all white, with round, wide eyes, tense. Second whistle. My mother shouted all the curse words she never wanted me to say. Juan thought this was hilarious and started repeating them. Third whistle, which seemed endless. My mother got out of the car, grabbed at my door but couldn't open it, screamed: 'Unlock it!' and I obeyed her immediately; I knew that when her forehead went wrinkly I'd better do what she said. So I did it. She opened my door, unbuckled my seatbelt, pulled me out of the car so hard I lost a shoe, and dragged me behind the car without ever letting go of my hand. Fourth whistle, short, and then a fifth and a sixth. My mother pulled at the door on Juan's side. It was locked. She told him to unlock it. He looked at her still smiling, but he didn't do it. My mother shrieked: 'Open this door right now!' Juan didn't know what it meant when my mother's forehead went wrinkly and she screamed with her eyes almost closed. I banged at the window. And for a second it seemed like Juan was going to open the door, because he reached out and touched the lock, but he didn't pull it up. My mother ripped at the handle again, banged on the window, shouted desperately at Juan through the glass: 'Open the door!' But Juan was so scared now that he couldn't obey. He started screaming and kicking, not even looking at us. It was impossible to make contact with him. Without letting go of me, my mother grabbed at the front passenger door, but it was locked too. 'Open the door, goddammit!' she shouted in vain at the little boy who couldn't even hear her any more. Then, finally, she accepted that Juan was never going to unlock the door. In a last desperate attempt, she pulled me back behind the car intending to unbuckle Juan and drag him out through the other door whether he liked it or not. We didn't make it in time. My bare foot got hooked on the rail and that slowed us down by a few seconds, until my mother tugged at me so hard my big toenail was ripped off. I screamed in pain; my mother saw blood, raw flesh, the nail pulled back, but she couldn't stop to console me, she just kept moving. With an urgency that I now understand. She gripped my hand tighter and pulled me along behind her, but just as we were about to reach my door, we heard a final, endless whistle. A whistle that I still hear, echoing through my nightmares. Then a crash. My mother and I were knocked to the ground. And from there, lying together beside the tracks, I watched as the train crushed our car. With Juan, my friend, inside. The car was squashed into a ball, swept down the tracks under the wheels of the train. Until it finally stopped. And my mother, as if waking from a trance, finally reacted. I didn't see what happened after that because she hugged my face to her chest so tightly I couldn't move. 'My toe, Mama,' I said. All I could say was 'my toe'. I said it over and over. She couldn't respond because she was sobbing inconsolably.

I write about that day over and over. For many years now, I've been searching for the words to recount this fragment of that day. I've perfected the story over time. What started with a few words, brief sentences, barely a paragraph, gradually became this text. I know what happened, I was there. I've added to the story little by little as I remembered colours, heard the alarm I hadn't paid any attention to that day. But even before, when I was still missing some details, or the words to describe those details, I always knew what had happened. I understood both then and now everything my mother did that day. I understand her desperation, her futile efforts. I also understand her errors in judgement, which conspired with fate. The train crushed our car with a little boy inside. I understand her fatal mistake. I think about what I would've done in her place, and I understand. The confusing messages sent by a railway crossing signal that never works. The terrible injustice of my mother's car stalling in that precise instant marked by misfortune. I understand that my friend couldn't comprehend the urgency of what was happening and then entered into a state of panic that kept him from unlocking the door. I understand why my mother opened my door first and then tried to open the other one. I understand the entire chain of events leading up to that accident and to Juan's death. I'll be forever haunted by the sound of that never-ending train whistle, the image of my friend kicking and screaming, the smell of scorched iron, my mother's horrified screams, her embrace so tight I could barely breathe, the pain of my big toe stripped of its nail.

I understand all that.

What I'll never understand, even if I write this story – my story – a hundred, a thousand times, is why my mother left me.

Why, after having gone through all this together, my mother left one day and never came back.

The Kindness of Strangers

WHY

Do I deserve to explain why? What I mean is, do I have that right? The right to unburden myself and expect someone to listen?

Certain actions can't be explained away. There are some things that no logic can justify. Maybe abandoning a six-year-old child is one of them. Unjustifiable. There's no possible explanation, no valid rationalization. That's why I remained silent all these years: I didn't feel I had the right to explain what drove me to do what I did because no reason or excuse would cover it. But I was just made to understand, after all this time in silence, that it's not about my right. It's about his right, my son's. We don't necessarily get to decide when to withhold our truth, when to keep it to ourselves. We do not always get to own our silence. He wants to hear it, so I have to say it. My version of events does not belong to me alone. Only I can give it. Only I can deny it. But denying it would be another mistake, a further misfortune, a new crime – depending on who's judging – which would only make everything I've already done even worse. My son wants an explanation. Even if that won't change the way he views my actions.

So I'll lock myself away this weekend which until recently I didn't know what to do with. Two free days between one week and another of work at Saint Peter's that initially terrified me. They still scare me, but for other reasons now. An entire weekend aware that my son knows who I am, aware that my son is somewhere nearby, and that he's aware of the fact that I'm here too. And I vacillate between action and paralysis. I don't rush out to search for him, I don't run to hug him, or cry with him, or let him insult me even, because before any of that, I owe him this explanation. And a proper explanation shouldn't be punctuated by sobs and insults, or even hugs. An explanation, or this one at least, requires so many words, too many, all the words I didn't say all those years I was absent. So I'll do what I have to do: I'll stay here and write.

But instead, I'm pacing around the apartment. As agitated as I was after first seeing him, inventing different excuses to keep from writing. To put off the pain of writing. The pain of searching for the words to describe this pain. I find myself wasting time on the perfect font, size, and margin width. I'm not going to write it by hand in this notebook, which I've been calling my 'logbook' – where I clipped my son's letter after stealing it from Federico Lauría's evaluation file. I'll type it on the computer I have here in the apartment, because I'm no longer writing for myself alone. When the text is finished, I'll print it and give it to him. And he'll read it, or so I hope. And even though I know that writing is all I have to do, I still don't write. I think about the form but not about the content. I procrastinate. I picked a title for the file. I'm calling it 'Why'. But I might come up with a better title later. I start to cry thinking about all these things – font, title, file – as the story rises up inside me, silently, waiting for me to gather the courage to tell it. But I can't. And instead of sitting down in front of the screen, I begin mentally reciting titles of novels. One leads to another. The book doesn't matter, the author doesn't matter, it doesn't matter if I like the novel or not, I'm not even sure if I read some of them. Just the titles, one after another, procrastinating, reciting them to keep from thinking about the task at hand, to stop my trembling. *The Wild Palms*, *The Grapes of Wrath*, *The Plague*, *The Corrections*. I notice that all of them start with 'the'. It's a useless fact, but I hold onto it and I try to think of other titles that start the same way. I focus on that, putting off writing a little while longer. *The Unbearable Lightness of Being*, *The Metamorphosis*, *The Hours*; in Spanish too: *El amor en los tiempos del cólera*, *El reino de este mundo*, *El Aleph*. In this way I manage to clear my mind for a few moments. To think without feeling. Why do I keep putting it off? Why can't I do it? I know I'm going to do it, I know I have no choice. But I'm still lost to procrastination. My Spanish students don't ever seem to worry about the titles of their essays and they often just use the prompt: 'Writing Exercise #1'. The teachers I have to evaluate don't think too much about how to title that final essay we ask of them either. They often call it just that, 'Essay'. Or 'Free Writing' or 'Essay by…' and then their name. That's what my son called his: 'Personal Essay by Federico Lauría.' I never correct those titles, neither with my students nor the teachers. But I know that choosing a title is an opportunity to give new meaning to a piece of writing. To this thing I still haven't written at this late hour on Friday night – almost three o'clock in the morning. I'd like my son to choose a proper title for that text he's written hundreds of times, the text I read today. First at the school, then back at the apartment. Over and over. Shaking. I think of possible titles. But it's not for me to decide, it's up to him. Sometimes, for writers, a title may come even before the first line, other times it might not emerge until the middle of writing, or only after the text is finished. When that's the case, when the title is added after everything has been said, it gives new meaning to what was written, modifies the origin a posteriori. Full understanding clicking into place at that moment. My son will only fully understand what he's written once he's able to find a title for it.

From the first line of that text I haven't started yet, I will force myself to write without holding anything back, to say everything there is to say, to forget that the reader is my son. To write for him, but as if I weren't writing for him. It would be unfair to put down anything less than the full truth out of fear of what he'll think. If I let myself think that I'm writing for my son it would have to be a letter, in the second person. But that would mean unavoidably omitting specific details, smoothing over certain circumstances, leaving out the parts that embarrass me. Things a mother wouldn't say to a son. Even if I am a very unconventional mother. That's what I was, in a way, from the first day I held Federico. I always thought of my son as someone older than he was, someone I could speak to like an equal, with whom I didn't need to use infantile, sickly-sweet language full of the diminutives and euphemisms that other mothers used with their children. He understood the way I spoke to him. Maybe because of that, at only six years old, he understood the seriousness of the situation when I asked him to unlock that car door. And Juan didn't. Juan was a little boy, and a little boy shouldn't have to face a situation like that.

I write – or I will write, as soon as I can – for an anonymous reader, any reader. Does a writer know who they're writing for? My students write, most of the time, for themselves; that's why – among other reasons – they'll never be writers. Once, at the Avenida de Mayo Teacher's College – where I started my degree but didn't finish – a professor once told us that Bertolt Brecht said he wrote for Karl Marx sitting in the third row of the theatre. I never found out if Brecht actually said that. Back then I'd never read or seen any of his plays – I only remember years later *Mother Courage and Her Children*, which Robert insisted we see together. Whether the Brecht quote was real or not, I always thought it would be intimidating to write for Karl Marx in the third row. As intimidating as writing for my mother in the third row. Or Mariano in the third row. Or my son. But, of course, I'm not a writer either. Merely a woman, a mother – am I a mother? – who must now write the story she went years without telling. And in order to do so I'll need to invent a reader different to the one who will receive this text and read it. If my son does in fact read it. Maybe all writers invent an anonymous reader so that they won't feel intimidated by the people they know will truly read it, truly judge it. A thought so intimidating it might even keep them from writing, cowed by the thought of exposing themselves to those people in that way. You imagine an anonymous reader because even though you know there'll be someone on the other side of the writing, it's better not to know who they are.

I still haven't started to write my explanation. I've solved the issue of the font, the title, the anonymous reader, but I keep putting it off. I read Federico's text again. And again. I don't know if I'm procrastinating for his sake or for mine. Or I do know. My son doesn't want my pity, he wants my reasons. I remained silent all these years for myself – because I didn't think I deserved to speak – now I have to speak, for him. To write. Without stopping. In this apartment in Temperley, I will take these two days to say everything I have to say. I just have to start. To put down the first word and keep typing until I reach the last one. That's what I have to do, now, in a few minutes, as soon as I can. To write. I stand up from the chair, I go into the bedroom, I rock from side to side in an exaggerated stretch, I throw my shoulders back, open my chest, align my bones.

And I look out onto the balcony. It's night-time. I know there's a bat making a nest and I won't let anyone trap her in there till she dies. I turn on the light. I find the place in the wood where I suppose her to be, I stare at that spot. I know she's here even though I can't see her.

Just like I knew my son was here, all these years.

Finally, I sit down at the desk, and I write.

Mariano and I married very young. We were both the same age: twenty-three. And we were in love. Or so we thought. Time teaches you that there's no one single definition of love. At that age it's very difficult to know this. At that age love is love, period. But often you fall in love not with someone, but with yourself in love. Or with what being in love implies, the positive side effects. You want to be in love, so you are. We were. We met one summer in Pinamar. He had a bunch of friends. I only kept in touch with a few girls from high school who I'd gone to the beach with for a few days. It was always hard for me to make friends, ever since I was a little girl. Sometimes I think it was because I didn't want to get close enough with anyone that I'd have to invite them over, let them meet my parents, view that suffocating, grey environment where my mother would regularly disappear between the sheets for days unable to get out of bed except to go to the bathroom, while my father hid behind a book on the terrace. To drown out the silence in the house, my father played Piazzolla records and taught me how to listen to them, helped me pick out the sound of the bandoneon among the other instruments, repeated the names of the songs for me every time, showed me how to move my hands in the air pretending to play my own bandoneon. My father tried hard to get me to enjoy that music that he considered to be 'of a superior quality', but he was disappointed when Piazzolla failed to mask my mother's silence.

'No, she's not crazy,' my father said with his habitual calm the few times I dared to ask, during one of those deep holes she fell into, 'don't listen to anyone who says that, they don't understand.' And then he'd go back to hiding behind one of his books or get lost in 'Oblivion', the Piazzolla song he reserved for the worst moments. I'd heard 'crazy' the first time from a distant cousin, at one of the few family gatherings we'd been invited to. 'Is it true that your mother is crazy?' But my father said she wasn't, and as far as I was concerned, if he said it, it was true. My mother wasn't crazy, but the fact that she wasn't crazy wasn't enough of an explanation. 'What's wrong with her then?' I wanted to know. 'She's sad,' my father answered, 'she gets sad sometimes, she's not always like that; your mother remembers every day, but remembering is one thing, the sadness only comes sometimes.'

I don't know why I never asked what it was that my mother remembered. 'Remember' used as a verb that required no object, simply 'remembering'. If my mother remembered, she got sad. Without an object. The sentence entered my head that way, textually, and was fixed forever: 'Your mother remembers.' And even though I couldn't do anything to help her, I felt in some way responsible for her sadness. As if I were to blame for my mother's remembering. Or as if I were capable of keeping her from remembering. Responsible for that objectless remembrance. What it was that caused her to sink into her bed every so often I only found out after the two of them, she and my father, were both dead. Federico hadn't been born yet, he was born two years after my mother died and a year after my father passed away. Sometimes I think uncovering that secret is what allowed me to get pregnant; before, even though we didn't use protection, it never happened. When my father died I had to clean out the house before turning it back over to the owners. Cleaning out a house, whether it's your own or someone else's, implies the risk of uncovering real ghosts, not-so-well-guarded secrets, of being devastated by some revelation, bowled over by an object that suddenly takes on new meaning. All that happened to me. I found out about a son – my brother. I finally understood what it was that my mother remembered: a baby she'd had before me. A baby who had a name: Gerardo, and a grave in the cemetery. There, among my parents' papers, was his birth certificate, his death certificate three months later, the receipts for the plot where he'd been buried stapled to a little card with a photo of the cemetery on the front and on the back a map of how to locate his grave. The grave of the brother I never had. The reason for my mother's sadness.

But it wasn't only my mother's sadness that kept me from having friends over. It was also because of my own self-consciousness, things that embarrassed me and I didn't want anyone to know about. I maintained a certain distance in my friendships so that they wouldn't expect to come over to have dinner with us, to sleep in my room on the worn-out mattress we kept under my bed, use the bathroom where, inevitably, and in spite of the many plumbers who checked the pipes time and again, it smelled like sewage. But even in spite of my own reluctance, I had a few friends I could plan a trip with. I wouldn't have been the first person they picked to join them but they weren't going to leave me out if I wanted to come along. I was one of those girls who never troubled anyone for anything, who was never a bother. Who no one remembered having seen at the party or not.

Why Mariano noticed me that summer was always a mystery to me. I know it helped that a few hours prior he'd been dumped by his girlfriend, Martha – a figure who always loomed large in our relationship, like Daphne du Maurier's Rebecca, immortalized by Alfred

Hitchcock. She'd dumped him to go backpacking with one of his best friends. She left him for the poorest guy in his friend group, the person he'd be most offended over being replaced by. So Mariano – or Mariano's ego – was obligated to move on as quickly as possible, to act as if he didn't care, as if he'd been waiting for that girl to leave him so he could fall in love with me – or with anyone, but I happened to be on hand, there, in Pinamar, staying in the same complex of beach bungalows, two doors down from his. I walked into the garden one afternoon, that afternoon, on my way back from the beach, and I saw him crying. It didn't seem at all strange to me. I'd seen my father cry many times even though whenever he realized I'd caught him he'd pretend it was because of whatever book he was reading. Mariano didn't have any book to hide behind. I looked at him, I didn't say anything, just looked at him, and he said: 'What are you doing tonight?' And that's how it all started, almost by accident. The next day he introduced me to his friends, he didn't say we were a couple but he held my hand, gave me kisses on the shoulder. I let myself fall in love with him because it was the first time in my life a man had ever seemed interested in me that way. I'd never had a serious relationship, nothing beyond games between kids that only went as far as a kiss on the lips behind some tree. My friends were jealous, they thought it was strange, so much love out of nowhere, they didn't trust it. I didn't tell them that Mariano's girlfriend had just dumped him but they figured it out somehow. 'He's just using you to save face in front of his friends, he's going to break up with you as soon as we get back to Buenos Aires.' But if he was in fact using me, I liked the way he was doing it. I liked it when he gave me kisses on the shoulder or ran his fingers through my hair, when he sang a song for his friends on the beach and said in front of everyone that he was dedicating it to me. One afternoon he got mixed up: he looked at me but he said Martha, and we all played dumb as if no one had noticed the mistake. It wasn't until the end of that trip, when Mariano had moved to rubbing me on top of my underwear, that my doubts fully vanished: I was in love with him, nothing else could explain the way I felt. And when we got back to Buenos Aires, in spite of my friends' pessimistic predictions, Mariano didn't break up with me. He invited me out to a bar near my house. I thought for sure he'd asked me out on a date so formally because he was going to break up with me. I imagined him saying 'It was fun while it lasted,' or some other meaningless expression meant to do as little damage as possible. But he didn't say that, instead he talked about us, about how he wanted me to come out to Temperley on the weekends because he couldn't stand the noise of Buenos Aires, that all his friends were there, how his house was big and I could have my own room, that he'd already told his parents about me. He asked if I'd told mine about him; I lied, said that yes, of course I'd told them all about him. 'You know my ex came back pregnant from her trip down south? What a mess, right?' And he welled up. But this time he didn't cry, at least not in front of me.

I never told Mariano what my friends thought about him, but it was clear that the dislike and distrust was mutual. Little by little I stopped seeing them as I made friends with Mariano's friends, his friends' girlfriends, his friends' brothers and sisters – Mariano didn't have brothers or sisters. I moved from a family of three in a grey apartment that smelled like sewage to a big family with aunts and uncles, cousins, grandparents. I'd always wanted a big family, I just didn't know it. It was an impossible dream, so it didn't even occur to me. My father had explained when I was very young that, shortly after

I was born, my mother had her first 'episode' and the doctors advised her not to have more children, so that's why I wouldn't have any new baby brothers or sisters. My father said 'new baby brothers or sisters' and I had no idea what the word 'new' hid. He also failed to mention that her first episode, a few months after I was born, coincided with the anniversary of the death of that baby that no one ever mentioned. But he did tell me that over time the few relatives we had in the first place began to distance themselves, stopped inviting us to their get-togethers, visited less and less often. 'It's their loss, when your mother is well she's nice to be around.' And it was true that my mother, in her good moments, could be a happy, fun lady, even affectionate in her own distant way, who liked to sing boleros and coerce clumsy rock-n-roll dance moves out of my father, who had no rhythm at all. The only Piazzolla song she allowed him to play, when she was well and came out of her room to live with us, was 'Libertango'. 'That one has some punch to it,' she would say, as she wiggled her arms and legs all around the house, like cracking a whip to the beat of the music. He and I never talked about the bad times, we acted as if they didn't exist and there was no chance they'd ever happen again; as if life was put on pause between one good moment and another. Selective amnesia is what permitted us to carry on with normal life. But, whether our relatives were wrong or my father was, we lost contact with them and I was raised in that tiny household of three, never daring to wish for anything more. Until that first Sunday I sat down at Mariano's table, which could fit twelve people comfortably, where everyone chatted happily and served themselves food or passed the wine, and I knew that this was what I'd always wanted: a family where food, conversation, laughter, and jokes circulated constantly from one end of a long table to the other. A dream that didn't last very long. Because I soon realized that large families can also be filled with resentment, lies, jealousy, and foul-smelling pipes.

I know that I fell in love with Mariano because I was attracted to him physically, because he was intelligent, because he was good at every sport, because he played the guitar and sang for me, because I'd seen him cry – although only that one time – because he desired me, because I liked feeling like I was in love. And because he had a big family. I don't know why Mariano fell in love with me. Assuming, after he got over the heartbreak of being dumped that summer, he did fall in love with me. I wouldn't have fallen in love with me. I asked him over and over: 'What made you fall in love with me?' And Mariano would respond: 'Everything.' But saying everything was like saying nothing. I was never able to get a specific answer out of him: your eyes, your smile, not even your tits, your legs. I'd have preferred him to say 'I fell in love with your tits' over that non-answer: 'Everything.' 'What made you fall in love with me?' Mariano would laugh; he thought the question was stupid. If he'd stayed with me ever since that afternoon in Pinamar when I saw him crying outside the beach bungalow, if he'd asked me to marry him, if he'd bought a house with a climbing rose for us to live in together, it had to be because he loved me, there was no further explanation required. And so I accepted that argument, I accepted that I was the lucky girl my mother said I was. But today I wonder if it isn't sometimes the other way around, first comes the desire for something: you want a house, a husband or a wife, a rose bush, so you fall in love – with whoever you can – in order to obtain those things.

We got married. As soon as Mariano found a house with a rose bush like his parents' house. I was halfway finished with my degree to become a teacher of Language and Literature at the Avenida de Mayo Teacher's College. Mariano convinced me to quit and finish at a different school in Lomas de Zamora. Saying that it was too far away, that it was a terrible commute, that I could use that time for something 'more productive'. It was the first time my father spoke up against something Mariano said, but I didn't listen to him. I dropped out of Avenida de Mayo. But I never graduated from the school in Lomas. I only finished my degree after Robert convinced me to enrol in a college in Boston and retake the classes I needed to get an equivalent degree. Not the same degree but something similar that would permit me to teach Spanish and Spanish-language literature.

The first years were like playing house. We would throw dinner parties for Mariano's friends who were now my friends. Or we'd go to dinner at their houses, or out to the movies, or card games: carioca, desesperado, asesino, basas, truco de seis. We were all playing house. If we had any money troubles, Mariano's parents helped us out. The salary his father paid him at the clinic was less than he could've made elsewhere, but his dad put gas in our car, paid our bills, took care of maintenance on our house. If we couldn't afford to take a trip, they rented an apartment in some beach town and invited us to join them. If we needed something for the house – dishes, a new TV set, a computer, or whatever – Mariano's parents would turn up that weekend with a bottle of the best red wine and the perfect present.

Until the first babies started to be born into the friend group. Then the game changed. We could no longer play house. A child was real, it cried for real, nursed for real, smiled for real, soiled its diapers for real. That was when we realized that life would never be the same. Up to then, we could pretend at anything, even pretend we were in love, but not any more. Some say that a family isn't complete until the second child is born, that after just one, all the members remain individuals. Maybe that's what happened with my father, my mother, and me. We never stopped being three individuals who lived under the same roof, aware of one other. This wasn't the case with Mariano's family, because there, the lack of a second child was made up for with an endless supply of cousins and other close relatives. Whether the theory is true or not, for us – Mariano and I – the sense that we were a family came with the arrival of our son. Maybe because we were used to families of three, maybe because we'd both always wanted a family more than a relationship. Maybe because when I finally discovered the source of my mother's sadness, I held onto that pregnancy tightly, convinced that if I didn't want it enough, if I didn't take care of it as well as I should, if I wasn't a good mother, the best, I would turn out to be some sad woman constantly remembering a son that no longer existed. In a way, that's what ended up happening. Whatever the reason, and without ever saying it, we both understood that we wouldn't have any more children. And we didn't.

As our relationship gradually faded, Federico became the centre of our lives. And the lives of his grandparents, great aunts and uncles, since he was the first baby in the family. Everything Federico did was celebrated. He was funnier than any other kid. More intelligent. His eyes more beautiful than any other pair of eyes. On a trip to Mar del Plata, when we stopped at a gas station, Federico saw a dead baby bird. He could only say a few words, he was just over a year old, but he saw the bird, pointed to it, looked at us and said: 'Birdie dead Papa Mama.' The entire family retold that story, they called each other on the phone to laugh about it, they repeated that sentence a thousand times at family gatherings. 'Birdie dead Papa Mama.' All it took was a 'Birdie dead Papa Mama' to conclude that the boy was clearly gifted, that his future was bright, that this child would stand out amongst the immeasurable crowd of other boys and girls.

Our son was the most intelligent, the most beautiful, the most loving, the most agile, the best, without a doubt. Until he started nursery school. Nursery school put our family to the test for the first time. In school, all his classmates seemed to their parents to be the most beautiful, the most intelligent, the best. Twenty-five kids in the classroom, all of them the best student. Even though they didn't know it, because it wasn't the kids having the debate – at least at that point in their lives – but the parents. A fierce competition began, testing the mettle of each family and their ability to accept their assigned place: second-best, middle of the road, forgettable, or worst of all. Federico had said 'Birdie dead Papa Mama,' but another classmate, over his plate of milanesa, said – at least according to his mother – that his dinner was shaped like South America. And another even more gifted child knew the capitals of all the countries in Africa. One kid had asked his mother if they could report the PE teacher for mispronouncing the name of the school in English. For every anecdote one parent told, someone stepped up to top it. Always. Every sentence uttered by one kid was met with a more advanced phrase; every drawing with a more creative one; every display of playground prowess with a yet more skilful one. When Federico started school, I was forced to face the cruelty and competitiveness of the world for the first time, the pressure to always be the best.

But my son starting school also gave me a healthy dose of humility. At the first parents' meeting I had to sit in a little chair the size of a toddler's butt, which mine spilled over the sides of. The teacher introduced herself and gave us a ball of yarn. We had to each say our names as we wound up or unwound the ball of yarn – I don't remember which. 'We want you to feel exactly what your children feel,' the teacher said, and I nodded my head even though I didn't have the foggiest idea how a kid just starting nursery school could feel like a dumb adult unwinding a ball of yarn with their big butt perched on a tiny chair. I wound up the yarn and said: 'I'm Marilé Lauría, Federico's mama,' and I was about to pass the ball along but before I could hand it off to the father sitting beside me – who couldn't lean forward enough to grab it because he was stuffed too tight into the tiny chair – the teacher asked me: 'What do you do, Marilé?' And I responded: 'My husband owns the clinic three blocks from here, on the other side of the station.' I wasn't the only one, many of the women in that first meeting introduced themselves as 'so-and-so's mama', or 'so-and-so's wife'. No man introduced himself as 'so-and-so's husband'. No one seemed to notice that we introduced ourselves this way. I didn't either at the time. Today I would, because I know that my last name is not Lauría. It never was. I use Robert's last name professionally because it's easier than my father's last name, Pujol, which everyone would mispronounce in Boston, butchering it, with u and j sounds that are wildly different in English. Although I have to admit that I also use Robert's last name because I feel that it's mine. Of that woman he first met, devastated over abandoning her son, there was nothing left, not even a name.

And nothing is all she would've ever had if she hadn't met Robert Lohan.

Federico was – maybe still is – the kind of person that everyone liked. His classmates fought to have him over after school. The mothers did too because they knew that inviting him over was easier than being alone with their children. He was never the best student in class – and that came as a blow to Mariano as soon as the first report cards came out: our son wasn't the best even though he'd said 'Birdie dead Papa Mama.' But he also wasn't one of the worst and at the end of the year he got the good citizenship award. Everyone liked being around him. I did too. He was great company for me. An equal, despite his age. I always spoke to him using adult language, he always responded with the same language, calling things by their names: vagina was vagina, penis was penis, death was death. When I found out I was pregnant with him, I felt shocked at first, paralyzed, frozen. Mariano jumped for joy as I sat there terrified. I didn't have anyone in whom to confide my lack of joy, my reservations. I didn't have close girlfriends to tell such private things to, or at least I didn't allow myself to. My parents were no longer alive, and even though I couldn't have spoken openly with them about my doubts, I longed for their presence, to have them there with me. I pretended to be happy, I should've been happy if I were a 'normal' mother. For the first time, at four weeks pregnant, I asked myself, in total solitude, if I truly wanted to be a mother. I'd never asked myself that question before. Why had I never asked myself? Why do some women take motherhood as a given? Why do we believe that it will come as naturally – and irreversibly – as winter turns to spring? But I did want that future child, I was certain, and when he was born I knew that there was nothing else in the world I could love as much as him. But despite loving that little boy, did I want to be a mother? Was there anyone in the world capable of understanding me, capable of comprehending that ambivalent feeling: loving your son, loving him deeply, while harbouring doubts about being a mother? And that question led necessarily to another: was I even capable of being a mother? Could I handle it? I was physically able to engender a child inside my body, to provide the conditions for him to develop during those nine months, give birth to him, but would I be able to care for him, to raise him once he and I no longer shared the same body? Or, like my mother, would I be just another person in a shared house, sometimes present and sometimes not? Would I only hurt that person I loved most in the world? Or could I learn to be his mother? My mother had her first episode after I was born, on the anniversary of the day her other baby, my brother, had died. Would the same thing happen to me? Would I be lost to the same darkness as my mother after giving birth to this child, even though I hadn't lost one previously? The doctor said no, Mariano said no. But I couldn't be certain until my son was born.

So many questions posed in solitude. Maternity is either taken as something automatic and irrevocable or it generates too many questions. It was because of these doubts that when Federico was born I handed him over to Mariano immediately: to protect him from me, to take care of him. It was a physical reaction, they put him on my chest but as soon as I finished nursing him I held him up and handed him to his father. I was afraid to touch him, to hold him in my arms, worried that he would slip through my fingers, that I'd hurt him somehow. Only after a few hours, once I'd made sure that I could stay there, saw that I hadn't left, that I hadn't been lost to sadness like my mother, was I able to hold him. But I always remained attentive, alert, fearful that one day I might turn into something else. A dark woman, like my mother. I spent six years with him and that fear never subsided, but it also never came true. Maybe life could've gone on that way if I hadn't had to cross the railway tracks with the barrier arm down that afternoon, to cross with the arm down like everyone else in the neighbourhood did since we knew it never worked properly. But life put that situation in my path. It doesn't happen to everyone, there are people who are born, live their whole lives, and die peacefully without anyone or anything ever testing who they are, what they're made of, what they're prepared to handle. Most mothers, for example, never have to go through such terrible circumstances to prove they can be a mother. But life decided to test me, and I, in so many ways, failed.

The months leading up to my leaving home were another test. I knew I was hurting my child by leaving, but by staying I might hurt him even more. If that tragedy had never entered our lives, that horrific situation of a lowered railway crossing arm and a car stalled in the middle of the tracks with a train coming, I'd have passed the test like so many other women. I'm not saying I'd have got the best marks, maybe just barely squeaked by. But I'd have been there, being the only mother I could be. Motherhood is full of little failures that pass unnoticed. If the circumstances had been different, no one, not even me, would've ever known who I could become.

Some mothers have all the luck; life never puts them to any kind of test.

I only have a little luck.

That year, the year Juan died, they'd chosen Federico to play Manuel Belgrano in the Flag Day celebrations on June 20. All it meant was he had a few more lines than the other kids in a little skit, and he'd have to hold the flag as they chorused 'I promise', after the teacher read the words that Belgrano himself read to his army of real soldiers, not primary school children. Federico was happy to get the part but he didn't make a fuss. He only told me when I asked: 'So, who did they pick to play Belgrano in the play?' 'Me,' he answered. It was the same question I'd always asked ever since preschool whenever I knew a performance for some patriotic day was coming up – before that, in nursery school when the kids were two and three years old, we hadn't yet figured out the whole thing about being picked for the plays. And up to now the answer had always been the name of some other classmate. The founding father changed, but Federico was never picked for the starring role. He was never Belgrano, never San Martín, never Sarmiento, never Columbus. Not the wizard in *The Wizard of Oz*, not Mowgli in *The Jungle Book* or Peter Pan in the end-of-year musical. He never got the part of any villain either – the leader of the Spanish Royalists, Captain Hook, the terrible Bengal tiger Shere Khan, characters who, although they were the bad guys, were still major parts, important enough to warrant inviting grandparents, aunts and uncles, or godparents to the play. Five years at that school, some thirty different plays that we showed up for, applauded, took pictures and videos of even though Federico had barely any lines beyond some random word – at best – and where they parked him in the back row, almost hidden in the wings. But none of that mattered any more because now, at six years old, our son had been given, finally, a starring role in the school play. Back then Federico was 'our' son. Ever since I left, I never again said – even to myself – 'our son'. As if Federico could either be Mariano's son or my son, but not both of ours together.

I knew that Gastón Darlin's mother had raised a fuss because her son had been hoping to play Christopher Columbus in the October 12 play the year before. And Betina Mendoza's mother complained because they'd made her daughter play one of Cinderella's ugly stepsisters while a classmate – who she considered to be clearly less attractive than her daughter – got the starring role. Also, in kindergarten, there had been a big scandal when Mateo Quirós's father burst into the staffroom yelling that making his son and the other boys wear turquoise pantyhose for the musical 'would turn them all gay'. And in the end, Gastón was assigned the part of Rodrigo de Triana – who had way more lines than Columbus with his famous 'Land ho!' – Betina got to play Cinderella, and none of the boys, especially not Mateo Quirós, had to wear turquoise pantyhose in the end-of-year musical.

Mariano demanded that I go and speak with the school. 'What's going on? What do they have against him? Is it because all the other mothers go up there to complain while you and Federico just sit there not making a peep, taking whatever comes, or doesn't come?' That year I swore to Mariano that I'd brought it up in the meeting I'd had with the teacher at the beginning of the year, that she'd assured me she'd keep him in mind, that she'd promised he'd have an important part in an upcoming play. But it didn't happen. So when Federico said he'd be playing Belgrano on Flag Day, we celebrated. 'You see, all you had to do was speak up,' Mariano said to me right in front of Federico, who looked at me and asked: 'Speak up about what, Mama?' And I answered, 'Nothing, son.' But Mariano, like he always did when he wanted to give us some life lesson, crouched down, took Federico's chin in his hand, looked him in the eye, and said: 'About injustice, son, you always have to speak out against injustice.' And the conversation ended there.

The incident at the railway crossing was three weeks before the Flag Day play. Federico told me a little about the rehearsal that day when he got in the car. He said that the hardest part was holding the flagpole up for so long because it was very heavy. But immediately Juan started singing the spider song and then Federico cut his story short and joined in. My son and Juan sang the spider song, a song that would haunt me for a long time afterward. 'Incy Wincy spider...' We were going to the movies. I didn't usually make plans during the week after school, Federico was always tired by that time of day and I was too, but I'd promised him. I'd arranged it as a treat mostly because Federico had got the starring part in the play, or because his father was happy because his son had got the starring part in a play, or because I was happy because his father was convinced that I'd managed to speak up 'against injustice'. But the official version for Federico and Mariano was that I was taking him to the movies in the middle of the week to celebrate the fact that he'd got first place in the painting contest that the art teacher had organized. Slowly, the little wins were adding up and I could compete with the other kids' successes when I went for coffee with the other mothers after dropping our children off in the morning. 'So he won the splatter paint contest? Maybe he'll turn out to be an artist, Marilé.' And, even though I'd seen my son's painting and I didn't think it looked much better than the other ones, I said: 'Yes, Federico has an artistic streak.' Those coffee hours were plagued with comments like this. And either criticism or praise of the teacher, depending on how marvellous she thought each of our children to be. 'She can't keep up with the kids, they're smarter than her.' 'She sized my little one up right away, she thinks he's brilliant.' 'He misbehaves because he's so bored.' 'Did your son tell you how badly the music teacher treated him the other day in front of the entire class?' Sometimes, not often, the conversations edged into more personal territory. One of those times I played the starring role. Or Martha. 'Did you hear that Martha moved back to town and her kids are on the waiting list for Saint Peter's?' 'Martha who?' asked a woman who was new to the group, but no one answered. But the one who'd shared the news looked at me and said: 'You don't care, do you? It's been so long…' The question took me by surprise. Why would I care about that woman who dumped Mariano on the beach in Pinamar to take off with another guy? But, even though I played it cool in front of the other mothers – even lied to myself – it did in fact bother me to hear that she was back. Her unspoken presence was always there between Mariano and I, someone we never mentioned but who echoed through our everyday actions – from preparing meals to having sex – as if Mariano was constantly comparing me to her. Or to what he imagined she would've been like had he married her instead. But I was the only one who knew about Martha's influence on my marriage – I thought – so I said: 'No, why would it bother me?' No one answered, someone changed the subject, and it seemed like we wouldn't have to talk about Martha any more, when another mother added: 'She moved back because she got divorced, the ex stayed down there. Where was it that they lived? Bariloche or La Angostura?' She said it like a passing comment and not as a response to my question, which was supposed to be rhetorical. But she was in fact answering me. She was saying that it should bother me, Martha was back and she was single. The other mothers nodded because they already knew and I realized that everyone except the one who'd said 'Martha who?' knew about her history with Mariano, which predated me and, in some way, they felt sorry for me. 'You don't care, do you?' one of the mothers asked again, I don't remember which one. I said that no, not at all. Not at all, I repeated and we changed the subject. Then the next time we got together for coffee Martha was sitting with us announcing that she'd managed to get spots for her kids at Saint Peter's, talking about her divorce, about how bad her marriage had been, going into great detail about her two sons: Pedro and Mariano. When she said 'Mariano', I took a sip of my coffee, trying to pretend that I hadn't even noticed the coincidence. But we all noticed. The silence that followed her son's name – my son's father's name, her ex-boyfriend's name – was awkward. But it didn't last twenty-three seconds thanks to Leticia Saldívar, who spilled a cup of coffee. And our shock was dispelled by that random clumsiness. Assuming it was random.

That afternoon we were going to the movies to celebrate Federico winning the art contest and we had just enough time to get there for the start of the feature presentation. We wouldn't get to see the previews, which was fine, but we wouldn't have time to buy choco-late-covered peanuts either, which was a shame, since for both of us, Federico and I, the movies without choco-late-covered peanuts just wasn't the same. Maybe I could set them up in their seats and go and get some. We'd have to see. When I got to the railway crossing there were two cars in front of me. That barrier arm – everyone who lived in the area knew about it – rarely functioned properly. That's why, very carefully, looking both ways, we always drove around it even when it was down. To the right was the station and it was easy to see whether there was a train coming from that way or not. To the left, however, some two hundred yards down, the tracks began to curve. That made a much larger margin for error. You could only be sure that no train was coming in the next two hundred yards, giving you enough time but just barely to zigzag around the barrier arm and cross the tracks. You had to do it quickly, not too quickly, but without hesitation. And you could never stop, ever.

But that was supposing that not stopping on the tracks was something the driver could control. And in this case, it wasn't.

It was not something I could control. But I was responsible. It was my fault.

I shouldn't have tried to cross the tracks.

But I did try to cross the tracks. And the car stalled.

And a boy died.

And there was nothing I could do to stop it from happening.

If the showing began at five-thirty, the movie itself would start about ten minutes later. We walked hand in hand, happily, down the sidewalk from the school to the spot where I'd parked. I didn't usually pick Federico up in the car, I usually walked to get him. But that day we were going to the movies, and the cinema was on the other side of the station, about ten blocks away. We'd just left school when Juan Linardi, one of Federico's classmates, came running up and pushed Federico from behind, making him stumble forward and almost tripping me. Despite the brusque push, Federico and I kept holding hands. A few steps behind came Juan's mother, laughing, I don't know why, and she said 'Wow, son, love that enthusiasm!' And then she added: 'Juan wants to invite Fede over to play at our house. His brother went to a friend's so they'll have the house to themselves. We'll bring him home after.' I didn't like the way Juan had pushed Federico. I didn't like that his mother didn't apologize for her son's aggression and instead thought it was funny. I didn't like that the woman had called my son 'Fede' – a nickname I never used – and I didn't like that she took it as a given that if her son wanted Federico to play at his house, my son would automatically comply. I tried to slow my breathing and prepare myself to calmly explain that no, Federico couldn't go play at anyone's house. But I didn't have to say anything, my son answered first, he said no, that we were going to the movies. Juan threw a fit. He was hyperactive and he always got upset when someone told him no or he didn't get what he wanted. Not worse than many other kids that age – or maybe a little worse, as several of the other mothers avoided inviting him over because they said he broke everything he touched. In any case, I found his behaviour especially jarring because Federico was such a docile child. As we stood there watching Juan kick the rubbish bin, furious that things weren't going his way, and I kept apologizing to the mother because we'd made plans to go to the movies days ago and we didn't want to cancel them, the woman opened her purse, removed her wallet, pulled out a bill, and handed it to me, saying: 'What if you take him to the movies with you? Even better, right? This should be enough, shouldn't it?' Federico looked at me and I knew what he was thinking, but I couldn't say no, I didn't know how to. It was all I could do to refuse the woman's money. The mother thanked me with exaggerated gratitude, kissed her son, gave him a big hug, told him 'behave' wagging her index finger in the air, and walked away. Juan, after shaking his mother off, smiled widely and slipped his arm around Federico's back, gripping his shoulder tightly like they were old friends. My son seemed to accept the situation with his usual compliance – a trait which was very convenient to everyone around him but which must've demanded a great effort on his part. I took Federico's hand again – Juan pressed up against him – and I walked them to the car. The same car that a few minutes later would stall on the railway tracks.

In which precise moment did it become inevitable? If life is a succession of events occurring one after the other, which of them, if they hadn't happened, could have stopped that tragedy from occurring? I'm not talking about the concrete and indisputable mistake of having crossed the tracks with the barrier arm down. I'm talking about something more subtle: destiny versus free will. I'm the one responsible for the tragedy. I always knew it, I never denied it. But my lack of caution had dramatic consequences; many other people had done the same thing and suffered zero consequences. So why did it happen? Why did it happen that day when we were with Juan and not any other day? Why did it happen to me and not another of the many drivers who crossed when the arm was down? Why did my car stall and not one of the cars that crossed right before us that very afternoon? Why did Juan die and not me? Why not Federico? And when I think about that, when I ask, or I write: 'Why not Federico?' my stomach does a flip. Like Juan's mother's stomach must have flipped when she found out that her son had died. She must've cursed not only me but also herself a thousand times over for insisting that her son come to the movies with us. Small actions no one would ever think twice about unless they set off a chain of events that ends in tragedy. If Federico hadn't won the painting contest. If the movie theatre hadn't been showing any movies that interested us that afternoon. If Juan hadn't thrown a fit about not coming with us. If his brother hadn't gone to play at his friend's house. Or if his mother hadn't been pushy and insisted that we take him with us. Or if I'd heeded Federico's imploring look and been bold enough to say no, that Juan couldn't come with us. I could've made up some excuse, or even just said no without giving any reason. If these factors or any others had been different: choosing another route, crossing the tracks at a different spot, leaving school five minutes earlier or five minutes later. I tortured myself with these questions for so many years. Until Robert helped me learn to accept it: the past can't be changed, there's no escaping it, no way to avoid it no matter which variables are altered. No shortcut, detour, or extra stop, no rhyme or reason. Just like you can't truly ever explain wars, massacres, plagues that decimate entire populations, or terrible illnesses in newborn babies. Why. What for. What's the reason for it. There's no answer. There's no escaping. The road map of my life included an unscheduled stop at that station and so it happened. The only thing that isn't fixed, Robert said, is what each person will do next. That's where free will comes in: what happens after the event, the accident, the war, the catastrophe, the mistake, the fatality. You couldn't avoid it, that wasn't an option, but you do have the chance to decide what you'll do next. And I decided. I didn't make the best choice, according to Robert. But I did choose. No one forced me to do what I did. Not everyone is able to choose the best option, not all of us are prepared to. But, according to Robert, we have the rest of our lives to keep choosing, to either repair a mistake or forever seal off any chance of repair.

The conversation with Juan and his mother ate up some of the little time we had. I helped the kids in, made sure they put their seatbelts on, and told them: 'Lock your doors,' I'll never forget that. At that time car doors – except the most sophisticated ones – weren't controlled by the push of a central button the driver could use to lock or unlock all of them at once. Instead, every passenger had to lock or unlock their own door. My car didn't have that kind of button, it was a basic model that was already several years old. Mariano wanted to trade it in for something newer but I thought it an unnecessary expense considering how little I used the car. I found it excessive that we had two cars for one household in the first place. That day, I didn't only say 'Lock your doors,' but when I got in, after putting on my seatbelt and starting the car, I checked: 'You locked your doors, right?' Juan didn't answer, he just started to hum 'Incy Wincy Spider,' and Federico said: 'Yes, Mama,' annoyed but also knowing it was better to answer so I wouldn't keep asking the same question forever. And he started telling me about the rehearsal.

If I hadn't said: 'Lock your doors.'

If they hadn't done it.

If another route.

If another theatre.

If another mother.

After the delay caused by Juan and his mother, I knew we were even more pressed for time to find a parking spot outside the theatre, buy the tickets, and get to our seats. Traffic was normal, we'd get there just in time. But the barrier arm was down. It never worked properly. Why didn't I think of it, why did I count on that luck my mother said I had. In the southern suburbs they'd just begun installing the first automatic barrier arms and this crossing had not yet been modernized. The railway employees, faced with staff shortages, gave priority to the crossing at the main street, which had more traffic. We'd been dealing with the situation for a long time and those of us who lived in the neighbourhood – or who simply had to drive through the area – felt we had the right to cross even when the arm was down. As if that recurring deception – the fact that the light blinked, the alarm bell rang, and the arm stayed down even when there was no train coming – led us to conclude that a train would never come no matter what.

Something like what happens in the tale of the boy who cried wolf. Only this story ended not with a liar eaten by a wolf but with a little boy run over by a train.

The barrier arm was down. There were two cars in front of me. Even though the bell was dinging and the red light was blinking I supposed that, like always, it was another false alarm. I cursed myself for having taken this route instead of the other one – and I never imagined how many times I'd curse myself for it later. I looked in the rear-view mirror with the intention of reversing, taking a different street and crossing at the other crossing. But just then a truck pulled up behind me and it was no longer possible to undo that decision. The first driver inched forward, nosed his way around the barrier, verified that it was a false alarm, and crossed the tracks. In the back seat the boys – my son and his friend Juan – sang a song in English that I'd never heard before. 'Where did you learn that song?' I asked them. But instead of answering me they continued singing. They must've learned it that day, pronouncing the lyrics like they had no idea what they meant, the music of one sound after another, the melody giving it a possible meaning independent from what it said. When they got to the pause of the second verse Federico asked me to look at them. I used the rear-view mirror to see how they moved their little fingers in the air as they sang imitating the movement of a spider, Incy Wincy spider. That melody, the sound of the lyrics, the gestures, the mispronounced words they didn't know in that other language, told them the story of the spider climbing up the drain pipe and resting there until the rain came to wash it down, once again, back to where it had climbed up from. Climb up and fall down and climb up again. Like Sisyphus, but a bug, and in English.

At some point, as Incy Wincy spider climbed up the spout again, I stopped watching Federico in the rear-view mirror and turned back to the road. I was alone in front of the barrier arm, the first car had disappeared, the second was manoeuvring around the arm to cross the tracks. A few seconds later it was gone. The two cars in front of me had crossed the tracks in spite of the blinking light, the bell, the lowered arm. I looked at the clock, the movie would be starting in five minutes. I had to decide whether to cross the tracks or not. And we always crossed. Everyone knew about that faulty crossing signal. I nosed forward, dodged the arm, and looked both ways. To the right, the station was clearly visible and I could see there was no train. I then looked to the left, but on that side I could only see for about two hundred yards because after that the tracks curved, blocking my view of what was coming. But those two hundred yards gave a car enough time to cross the tracks. Unless of course the car in question stalled on the tracks. And inexplicably, my car stalled. To this day I have no idea why. It wasn't anything I did – not pressing the clutch enough, or changing into the wrong gear, or accelerating too fast. Because I immediately tried to start it back up: I put it in neutral, turned the key in the ignition. But the car wouldn't start. I tried again but it still wouldn't start, tried a third time and again, nothing. That's when I heard the train whistle. I looked to the left and I knew, for the first time in my life, what panic was. Not fear, not worry, not even the word 'panic' used in everyday speech. True panic. I tried to start the car again, the sound of the train whistle making me even more agitated. The car made a raspy sound that fooled me into thinking, for a second, that it was finally going to start. But then the motor immediately died. I knew that the car wasn't going to budge. So I shouted: 'Take off your seatbelts!'

and I jumped out of the car to help the kids. I fumbled first at Federico's door. Beyond the fact that it was the side my son was on, it was the door I came to first. Juan's mother would later condemn me for that – not to my face, she never spoke to me again, but she made it known that she thought I'd 'chosen to save my son' – and others agreed with her. Although I can't prove it, I'm certain that if the kids had been sitting in opposite places I still would've opened that door first. It's logic, common sense, instinct. But I can't be certain and a case like this, with a child's death involved, demands certainty. You might be convinced that you know what you'd do in a certain situation, but you can't truly know until you're faced with it, until you're in that situation for real. Everything else is pure speculation. But it certainly seems absurd to go right past a door and not try to open it. So that's what I did, I tried to open the door I came to first, Federico's door. It was locked. I'd told them to lock their doors when we got in the car and checked that they'd done it. And even though when I got out of the car, I shouted 'unlock the doors!' the door was still locked. I shouted at Federico again, saying: 'Open the door!' And Federico opened it. I undid his seatbelt and pulled him out. Then I ran around to Juan's door dragging Federico behind me, pulling him by the hand, as if his body were an extension of mine. I shouted: 'Open the door!' But Juan didn't open his door. I shouted louder but that only had the reverse effect and instead of opening the door Juan got mad and started kicking the seat in front of him, one leg and then the other crashing against the passenger's seat, until he got tired, stopped, and started to cry. He cried like a little kid, because he was. I grabbed at the front passenger door, it was locked. I shouted again, 'Open the door!' I tried to say it more calmly but with the same urgency, with the same emphasis. Federico banged on the window with his little fist and repeated my words: 'Open up, open up, Juan!' But he said it without shouting, almost like a whisper or a prayer to himself. Juan was crying even harder, he started kicking again, his eyes fixed straight ahead on the seat in front of him. So many sentences to describe something that happened in so few seconds. Time expanded by words. Then Juan, still crying, looked at me, terrified, and I finally understood that he would never open the door. All I could do was go back over to the side Federico had been sitting on and pull him out that way. Why didn't I do that before, when I took Federico out? Because Juan was far enough away that I thought it would take longer to lean over and unbuckle him from that side, because I trusted that he'd unlock the door just like my son had, and because in these kinds of situations, evidently, people don't always make the best decisions. We ran behind the car. My son, who was missing a shoe – it wasn't until that moment that I realized he was missing a shoe – got his big toe caught in the tracks. He tried to free himself but he couldn't with me pulling from one side and the track from the other. 'Mama!' he said, 'I'm stuck!' and once again the train whistled, an endless whistle that I think must still be sounding. In my desperation to get Juan out of the car I tugged on Federico's arm so hard that he lost his toenail as his foot came unstuck. He screamed in pain, his toe was soaked with blood. But I didn't even consider stopping. Federico's blood, something that under normal circumstances would have made me want to faint, was the least of my worries at that moment, I couldn't even think about his blood, even look at it, I couldn't feel his pain, all I could do was get to the door I'd pulled my son out of and save his friend, another mother's son.

But I didn't make it. The train whisked the car away before I could reach the other door. With Juan inside it. The speed of the locomotive and the adjoining cars made such a huge impact that we were thrown backward onto the ground. Federico cried, saying: 'My toe, my toe, Mama.' His toe kept him from thinking about Juan as the train ran him over. Or at least from saying it, from naming him. The whistle kept blowing even after the train stopped. And underneath that sound we could hear the crunch of the metal being crushed. And the screams of the people waiting at the station.

I knelt down and pulled my son to me, I hugged Federico so tight that he couldn't turn to see what I was seeing: the car fully underneath the train, crumpled into a twisted ball, with a child inside.

I didn't go to Juan's funeral. After they took us to Mariano's father's clinic – I always found it hard to say 'Mariano's clinic' much less 'our clinic' – and the entire medical staff checked that we didn't have any physical damage beyond Federico's missing toenail and some scrapes and bruises, they sent us home. Me, sedated, Federico in the constant care of his grandparents or aunts and uncles. In my moments of lucidity I feared I was beginning to have episodes like the ones my mother suffered. Assuming she was suffering during those periods – like my father and I were – more than the other moments, the ones in which she had to live in the world. But once the effect of the sedatives wore off or waned between one dose and another, all I wanted was to see Federico. My only wish was to be with him, unlike my mother, who only wanted to be alone with her darkness.

I wanted to see my son, to hug him, to cry with him if necessary. But I could only see him in the presence of someone else – his grandmother, a great aunt, Mariano, or whoever – as if they were afraid to leave me alone with my child. One afternoon when no one was able to sit with us for a few hours, Mariano asked Martha to come over. She brought Pedro, her youngest, who was the same age as Federico and became friends with him as soon as he joined the class. They brought a present, a dinosaur with wings and a tail longer than its body. Federico unwrapped it and the boys started taking turns flying it around the living room like it was an airplane. After a while they took the game outside. I was left alone with Martha. She offered to make me a cup of tea. We both went into the kitchen. Martha had wanted to do it herself but I wouldn't let her; I didn't want her to seem like the lady of the house with me as the guest. 'You have to be strong,' she said to me and I felt like it was just a throwaway comment, something she or anyone else could've said. In fact several people had already said those very words to me after what had happened at the railway crossing and Maplethorpe himself would say the same thing a few days later, although with greater sincerity. 'You have to be strong,' coming from Martha, sounded like a cliché so I let it go in one ear and out the other. But then, as she filled the kettle and put it on the stove, she added: 'Because of what happened, but more importantly for what's going to happen now.' That made me sit up and take notice, 'And what is it that's going to happen now?' I asked. 'Well… You know what happened at Juan's funeral, Mariano must've told you.' 'Yes, he told me a little,' I lied. 'It was so horrible to see the mother screaming at him like that, saying such terrible things, kicking him out of the funeral…' I felt like the kitchen floor was tilting under my feet. 'He handled it with dignity… you would've been proud of him if you'd been there.' I looked down. My legs were shaking. Martha continued: 'Because, you know, what does Mariano have to do with any of this? And Federico, poor thing…' I stared at her, she was silent for a moment, her eyes fixed on mine and then she said, in a quieter voice: 'You neither, not the way she said it, of course…' As if trying to distance herself from that last comment, she checked to see if the water was boiling in the kettle, put teabags in each mug, and only then continued. 'It was an accident, it could've happened to any of us, we all cross when the arm is down, but you know how people are… That's why I'm saying that what's coming isn't going to be easy, because I already started hearing things, ridiculous things, of course, and you'll hear them too. I think it's better for you to be prepared. Because not even the strongest woman could stand hearing those comments. I wouldn't be able to handle it.' 'Things like what?' Martha turned the stove off, poured water into my mug, and placed it in front of me. 'Just certain comments, looks, insults.' 'Tell me what you've heard, so I can prepare for it,' I said. Martha looked at me, paused as if trying to decide whether to tell me or not, and then said: 'Well… if you want to know… Maybe it's better… Things like Mariano had been trying to get you to trade in that car for a while but you wouldn't, that you were always a very jumpy driver and that made you a dangerous driver, that you were on medication…' Martha turned her back to me as she made her own tea. 'That you sometimes seemed…' 'I wasn't on any medication,' I interrupted her. 'I know, I know… Mariano told me. But that's what they're saying. They're going to say a lot of things that aren't true. Things that sound plausible; you know how it is, the lie that sticks is the one that's built around something that could be true. If they said you were nervous because you were meeting a lover at the movies, no one would believe it. But that you were on medication is something believable, you might seem sort of sad or nervous sometimes, not always, but if they've seen you like that just a few times it's enough to build their theory.' Martha came to the table with her cup and sat across from me. 'Why wouldn't it be believable that I had a lover?' I asked. 'Oh, no, Marilé, I meant it as an example, don't take it literally. Anyway you don't seem like the type, just that, you can tell you're happy with Mariano. He's such a great guy, why would you cheat on him?' 'You cheated on him,' I said. Martha looked at me with a blazing bitterness that she couldn't hide. All afternoon she'd been feigning affection for me but this comment had loosened some spring and she wasn't able to pretend any more. She glared at me for a moment, finally showing her true self, as she really was. As she really is. And then she said: 'We were too young.' She stood up and found some cookies in a tin in the pantry, without asking for permission, as if it were her house. She arranged them on a plate. In the time it took she was able to compose herself. Her face relaxed and, as if I'd never made any reference to the fact that she'd cheated on Mariano, she picked the conversation back up where we'd left off. 'Someone even came up with a story that you had a family history of depression, that your mother had I don't know what kind of problem…' 'Who knows anything about my mother? Who even met her to be able to say something like that?' 'I don't know, I don't know… Look, you hear so many things I don't even remember who said what. Does it matter who it was?' For the first time that afternoon I agreed with something Martha said: it didn't matter who'd said it. 'And out of all these people giving their opinions on me, making assumptions about me, judging me, isn't there anyone on my side?' I said. 'No one asked how I'm doing?' 'Yes, yes, of course, that too, of course they asked. Even, look, you just reminded me, several of the mamas who knew I was coming to see you said to say hello. Of course many people are worried about you! But… well, they're also worried about what we're going to do now.' 'Do what now? What does that mean?' 'We're all having trouble imagining how we're going to handle seeing the two of you together.' 'Who?' I asked. Martha stared at me as if to say: you really don't know who I'm talking about? But she didn't say it and went on as if I hadn't asked. 'At the school events, at our coffee hour after dropping the kids off.' Martha said 'our coffee hour', already a part of the group even though she'd only joined us a few weeks back. 'If Juan's mother could say those things to Mariano at the funeral, are you prepared to run into her at the café, at school, at some kid's birthday party, and have her scream that at you?' 'Yes, I'm prepared to have her scream at me. I understand, I accept it. Her son died and I was driving that car. I think about them all day long. Her and her son. I cry for them. I dream about them. I wake up in the middle of the night hearing Juan's screams. I'm prepared to face her and let her say whatever she needs to say. Maybe the other mothers aren't ready.' Martha sighed: 'Well… it's going to be very hard for everyone. Very hard…' The door opened, Federico and Pedro came in pushing each other and laughing. 'Maybe it would be better if you met privately first, you and her. I don't know. Talk it over with Mariano to see what he thinks maybe,' Martha said as she picked up the teacups and rinsed them out in my sink.

I didn't answer, not only because I didn't have anything to say, but because just then Federico hopped into my lap and put his arms around me and I no longer cared what that woman had to say. Or what she didn't say with words but left floating in the air, more intrusive than the winged dinosaur she and her son had brought as a present.

As soon as they left Federico looked up, pointed his index finger at the ceiling, and said: 'Mama, is Juan in heaven?'

I said yes. Because there are moments when, even though you don't believe in heaven or life after death, it's better to lie.

I lied to him and I lied to myself.

That night I waited for Federico to fall asleep and then went down to Mariano's study to talk to him. After dinner he usually shut himself away in there to finish up work stuff – or so he said – for a couple of hours then he came up to bed. Before the incident at the railway crossing I would wait up for him watching TV or reading. But lately I had so much sedative in my system that I fell asleep as soon as I lay down. And if I woke up it was because Juan appeared screaming in the middle of my dream, despite the medication. I'd decided not to let the same thing happen another night so I didn't take the pill I was supposed to take with dinner and I waited up for him. Two hours later I began to worry he'd never come. I wondered if ever since the day our whole life had been crushed by the train he'd stopped coming up to our room altogether. Maybe he'd been sleeping in the living room without my having noticed and only came up to unmake his side of the bed a few minutes before the sedative wore off and I woke up. I tried to remember if Mariano had been there beside me all those nights I woke up thinking about Juan, but I couldn't picture him there.

I quietly left the bedroom, went downstairs, walked into his study, and only after I called his name, 'Mariano', did he look up at me. 'What's wrong?' 'Can we talk?' 'Now?' 'Now.' He didn't seem pleased at the prospect, but he set down his papers and looked at me. 'Martha was here.' 'Yeah, I know.' 'She told me some of the things people are saying.' Mariano didn't respond, he held my gaze for an instant and then looked back down to check something on the page he had in front of him. I kept going: 'She told me what happened at the funeral.' Mariano still didn't say a word but he started to pile up his papers with exaggerated movements, making it clear that I was keeping him from being able to work any more that night. But, ignoring what he was saying to me with those gestures, I kept going: 'I'm scared that everything they're saying is going to affect Federico. I don't want those nasty comments getting back to him when he returns to school next week.' My mentioning Federico, maybe, shook Mariano out of his silence. 'We need to let some more time go by, I don't think Federico is going back to school next week.' 'But he's fine,' I argued, 'and he wants to. Also he has to rehearse for the play. Flag Day is coming up and...' Mariano interrupted me: 'Federico isn't going to the Flag Day play.' I didn't understand. 'Why wouldn't he go?' 'He's not going,' Mariano said again, 'I already told the school.' I couldn't think clearly. I knew that before the incident at the railway crossing the entire family had celebrated the fact that Federico was chosen for the play. It was something we were all looking forward to and Federico loved going to rehearsal. Of course I knew what had happened but I didn't understand how that affected Federico's participation in the school play. I still had no clue what was going on. 'We can't disappoint him like that,' I said. Mariano looked at me with an expression I'd seen him make often but this time it was more condescending. It mirrored the way Martha had looked at me that afternoon. At the time I wasn't able to put a name to it, today I'd say that he looked at me as if thinking: 'Let's see if this woman can wrap her little brain around this.' This woman, or this idiot, or this idiot I'm stuck with. After a long, awkward silence, he said: 'It would disappoint him even more if all the mothers got together and asked the school to kick him out of the play.' I was shocked, the thought hadn't even crossed my mind. 'They would never do something like that,' I said. 'Yes. They would,' he answered, with a certainty that required no further explanation. But he explained anyway: 'In fact, Susana, Lucas's mother, told me they were planning to do just that. She said they'd all been talking and they thought the kids might get upset if they had to stand in front of Federico and say: "I promise."' And when Mariano said 'I promise,' his voice broke, his lower lip quivered for a second. He cleared his throat, covered his mouth and coughed two or three times. Then he went on: 'Maybe you forgot that Juan's brother is in the class that's going to be pledging to the flag.' I had forgotten that. 'She assured me that it had nothing to do with him, of course, but that Federico might remind them of the tragedy, that the flagpole might remind them of the railway crossing arm, that the image might bring the incident flooding back right there on the stage. And most of all because Juan is dead and we should respect the family. All that and some other things it's better not to even repeat.' 'Like what?' Mariano paused to once again give me his look of 'how is it possible this woman doesn't understand.' He didn't answer the question left hanging in the air and instead said: 'I think it's better not to stir up any more trouble, Marilé. Federico isn't going to the play and that's that. That's my decision.' My legs started shaking. I willed myself to remain standing but I didn't know if I could hold out very much longer. I didn't care about the play and my son being stripped of his starring role so much as that warning Mariano had received and what it meant for me going forward. 'Didn't you say it's important to stand up when something's unfair?' I asked, repeating his advice from a week earlier. 'In a case like this no one knows what's fair,' he answered. 'We'll let the play blow over. We'll let some time go by.' 'I don't want to, I don't think it's right, I think it's unfair, even if all the other mothers think differently. Why him? I can skip the play if necessary. Let them blame me if they want to, but not him.' 'Of course they're going to blame you. Everyone's going to blame you. They already do. In the worst way.' 'What do you mean?' 'Don't worry about it, I already took care of it. At least partly.' 'What do you mean?' I repeated and I felt like my teeth might crack from clenching them so hard as I waited for his answer. Mariano looked at me, but this time not with that expression I knew so well. Now he looked at me with a mixture of disgust and pity, a look that would've hurt me if all my pain hadn't already been focused somewhere else. 'What do you mean, Mariano?' I asked again. 'Juan's parents threatened to file a lawsuit, not just a civil suit but a criminal one as well, they came to see me. Do you know what "a criminal case" means?' He said it sarcastically, his way of emphasizing the fact that I had no clue what was going on. 'And?' I asked instead of answering. 'I managed to reach a private agreement with them,' he said and he got up to leave his office, effectively putting an end to our conversation. I didn't budge from where I was standing; if Mariano wanted to leave, he'd have to either move me out of the way or climb over me. 'I don't understand what that means,' I said. He stopped about a foot away, and answered: 'It means I paid them, Marilé. I paid them to keep you out of prison.' I shook my head; I couldn't say a word. I didn't understand why – even though I felt horribly guilty – I would ever go to prison. 'I paid them so they wouldn't sue you, so you don't end up locked away in some cell, but I can't pay them enough not to give you dirty looks, not to ignore you, and I can't pay them not to exclude our son either,' Mariano said, pushing me aside so he could leave the office.

I stood there for a second, gathering my courage, and then followed him up the stairs. 'What does Federico have to do with it?' I asked again, a few steps behind him, neither one of us stopping. 'Nothing, obviously. Federico has nothing to do with it, he's a victim too. But our son is a reminder of what happened and they can't stand it.' 'Not a reminder of what happened, a reminder of what I did,' I corrected him, saying what he was clearly thinking. Mariano stopped and turned to look at me. He was still disgusted but now without a hint of pity, and from where he'd stopped on the stairs he said: 'Enough, Marilé!' And that 'enough' sounded like 'don't make me say something I don't want to say.' Then he went into the bathroom and shut the door.

I heard the sound of the shower as I stood there frozen, on the same tread of the stair where my husband had just said to me: 'Enough, Marilé!' because he didn't dare to say what he really wanted to say.

Federico didn't go to the Flag Day play. He returned to school the week after. He was glad to go back and he came home happy every day. Until one day I noticed he seemed sad. I caught him looking up at the sky, looking for who knows what. When I asked him if he was all right he said, 'Yes, Ma, everything's fine.' He didn't say 'I'm fine' but 'everything's fine'. I knew perfectly well what was happening – and what he wasn't telling me – I could see the happiness had been wiped off his face, no matter how hard he tried to pretend so that I wouldn't worry.

With the excuse that it would be good for me to rest a little more before facing the thought of taking Federico to school, Mariano started driving him in the mornings. In the afternoons he rode home on the bus that dropped the Saint Peter's students off at their doors when their parents weren't able to pick them up. Some days Mariano told me Federico would be home late because he'd been invited to play at Martha's house. He wouldn't let me go to pick him up there, even though I could've easily walked. 'I'll bring him home,' he said. 'You get some rest.' But I didn't want to rest. I was exhausted from so much rest. I wanted to confront this thing that seemed increasingly menacing, ever darker. I wanted to face my fear head-on and vanquish it once and for all.

I was always alone. There are moments, circumstances, situations, mistakes, tragedies, that show a person who their true friends are. And once again I'd been shown that I didn't have any. A few mothers sent their regards through Mariano or Martha – the only adults I saw – one or two even called and we had a brief exchange of 'how are you', 'doing better', 'I'm glad'. My in-laws did what they always did when faced with a problem they couldn't solve using money: they exited the stage, came around as little as possible, shielded themselves. They took an extended trip. To Europe, a few days after Federico went back to school. I never even saw them again except for one or two visits at the clinic. They claimed it was a trip they'd had planned for ages, that they couldn't cancel because they'd arranged to meet different friends in different cities. Whatever the reason, they weren't around either.

I would've liked my parents to have been alive. To be part of that family of three, so strange to others and so safe to me despite our difficulties. I'd have given anything to spend a little more time in that place where I could weather any storm, even if the wind and the rain still blew in, getting just as soaked as I would outside, but consoled by things that were familiar and unconditional. My mother and father did only what they could and what they could was very little, but they were unconditional with me. Even though my mother spent so much time locked in her room, wallowing in misery, and my father spent hours hidden behind a book on the terrace, listening to Piazzolla. I would've liked for them to have met Federico, watch him grow, to see me as a mother. To be able to talk to them about what happened at the railway crossing, the hatred everyone showed me. Or at least the hatred I felt they had for me, based on what Martha and Mariano said. Whether they hated me or not. To talk about Federico. And that little boy, Juan, who came to me at night and who my son searched for in the sky. To work through my pain and my son's, my remorse over Juan's death. To banish the silence surrounding the brother I never met, whose existence I only learned of once they were gone. But none of that was possible: my parents were dead. And I was alone.

One morning I was surprised by a visit from Mr John Maplethorpe, the director of Saint Peter's. I was startled to see him at my door, afraid something had happened to Federico. 'Don't worry, I just stopped by for a visit.' I invited him into the living room, he sat down and smiled at me. All it took was that smile, the smile of a person I knew, who knew what had happened, not a friend or family member but simply a familiar stranger, to make my eyes fill with tears. Maplethorpe noticed, but we both ignored it. For as long as we could. He had a box of chocolates tucked under one arm. He sat silently for a moment before handing it to me. And then he said: 'Chocolate never hurts,' passing me the box. Then I couldn't pretend any more and I started crying. Maplethorpe moved his chair closer, took my hand, and squeezed it tightly. 'Cry if you need to,' he said, and I obeyed. I cried for a long time in front of the director of my son's school, until I got all my emotion out and finally caught my breath. It was a short but intense visit. He didn't say much, but he said just the right things, the things I needed to hear. He sat silently and had a cup of tea with me, as if the objective of his visit was just to provide me with some company, to be there, let me cry, hold my hand, give me consolation. And then he said: 'I came because I wanted to see you, to say hello, and most of all to hear from you how you're doing.' I didn't answer, thinking it was one of those lines that didn't require a response – just another throwaway remark like so many others – despite the fact that his kindness set him apart. And I also thought, even though I hadn't answered, that before he left he'd say: 'I'm glad to see you're doing well, you know you can count on me if you ever need anything.' But no. Maplethorpe wasn't a man for small talk or platitudes. Beyond the simplicity of the expression, he genuinely expected a response. He asked it again more directly, in a way that would not allow me to avoid answering. 'How are you doing, Marilé?' I looked at him and let out a long sigh. 'Good, doing better… thanks,' I said, even though we both knew that my answer was a lie. Maplethorpe took my hand again, squeezed it and gave me another smile. 'It's hard…' I added. And he said: 'Of course it is.' And he smiled again. Maplethorpe is one of those people who smiles more with his eyes than with his mouth. 'It will pass, in time,' he said. 'Not the memory, or even the pain, that will always be there, but it will hurt less.' And after a brief silence in which he never let go of my hand, Maplethorpe stood up to leave, but before he did so he stopped for a second to say: 'Don't let them define you, don't let them do that. Some communities are very insular, very…' – he searched for the word – 'judgemental. That's the word: judgemental. And a bit hypocritical as well, I have to say. People who don't know how to put themselves in other people's shoes. They point their fingers and pass judgement, certain that they'll never be seated in the same spot. Don't let them. You have to be strong.' And then Maplethorpe shook my hand in goodbye, and repeated again: 'You have to be strong, Marilé.' The same words Martha had said, but this time they were sincere and well-intentioned. Then he left.

As soon as I was alone, I went into my room, shut the door, and cried. But the tears were different. Hot, round tears rolled down my face because Maplethorpe's visit made me feel for the first time that someone truly cared how I felt, how I was doing. And even though he didn't deny my responsibility for the accident, he was able to put himself in my place, empathize with me. Maybe even forgive me.

Perhaps bolstered by Mr Maplethorpe's visit, or because enough time had passed, or just because, a few days after that conversation, when Federico was at school and I was trying to take a nap to get the rest everyone said would be so good for me, I decided I would get up and prepare to pick Federico up from school. I got dressed painstakingly. I didn't want my appearance, which I'd completely ignored since the incident at the tracks, shut up inside the house, to be interpreted as a sign of neglect or depression. I chose shoes that were uncomfortable but elegant and a skirt that I only wore to social events, birthdays, or special occasions. This was a special occasion, maybe. I walked to Saint Peter's School, without notifying anyone, with no plan in mind, spurred on by impulse, having made the decision that the time had come. I wanted to pick my son up from school, that was all, to watch him laughing and playing with his class-mates. I wanted to prove to myself that he was still living the happy life he'd had before the day we wanted to see a movie and instead ended up watching a train crush my car with his friend inside. I didn't care if the other mothers gave me dirty looks, or pretended not to see me. I didn't even care if someone came up and said to my face the things Martha had told me they were saying behind my back after school and at coffee hour. I just wanted to see Federico. To see him in his world, with those people. I hadn't decided if I'd go in to get him or just watch from the sidewalk across the street from behind a tree or a car. I just wanted to see him.

The walk from my house to the school was not easy. My shoes hurt my feet, I was out of shape, and my legs were exhausted after the first few blocks. Ever since the accident I'd only moved from one room to another inside the house. By the time I got to school I was out of breath and the kids had already been dismissed. I worried

Federico had left before I got there. I searched for him in the crowd of kids but I couldn't find him. Then I saw his classmates exiting the building in single file. They were being led by a woman. It was Ignacio's mother, one of the women I used to have coffee with. I looked for my son among them but he wasn't there. The kids were being shepherded by the mother and two teachers onto a bus decorated with birthday balloons. Only after everyone was on the bus and it started up did Federico come out of the school building. He was holding hands with Martha, followed by her own sons. There was no one left outside the school, no mothers, no students, no teachers. I walked up to them. 'What are you doing with my son?' I asked Martha. 'I was taking him home. Mariano didn't tell you he comes over to play in the afternoon sometimes?' 'Yes, but he didn't say anything today.' 'Because we planned it last minute. I called him a little while ago and we set it up. He's probably trying to call you at home to let you know.' 'You made him miss his friend's birthday…' I said. Martha gave me a complicit look that I didn't understand, and then leaned over and said quietly: 'I didn't make him miss it, Federico wasn't invited, Marilé. Pedro was, but I chose to keep him home so that Federico wouldn't be the only one who didn't get to go.' 'All his friends were there…' 'Yes, but Federico was left out, it's horrible. I did everything I could, I talked to Ignacio's mother, the teacher even called her too, but there was no changing her mind. She's very good friends with Juan's mother, who's going to be there, along with Juan's brother who's friends with Ignacio's brother. You have to understand, it's going to be difficult, it has nothing to do with Federico…' 'I know it has nothing to do with Federico. It has to do with me, so why do they take it out on him?' 'It's nothing to do with anyone, it's just the situation, this tragedy that's affected everyone. People are just trying to avoid uncomfortable situations while the kids are blowing out their candles, that was what she was worried about. They'll get over it,' she said, and then added, in a harder tone: 'Or not, we'll see.' And then she sweetened back up and said: 'Do you want to come over?' as if it were time to put the problem away so we could all march happily to her house for milk and cookies. 'No,' I said, 'we don't want to go to your house.' And leaving Martha standing there with an insulted look on her face, I left with my son, who'd been standing silently beside me all that time, squeezing my hand, almost pulling me away.

We walked for a while without a word. Federico stared at his shoes, as if measuring his steps, carefully choosing where to place each foot, calculating the distance. I wanted to pick him up, rub his back, hug him tight, let him cry on my shoulder and console him, to protect him from that undeserved mistreatment. But I didn't do it. I couldn't weigh Federico down with my sadness on top of everything else. Instead I tried to stay in step with him, imitating his movements, letting my son guide me, not the other way around. In this game and in life as well.

When we'd gone two or three blocks from the school, Federico pulled at my arm and said: 'Ma…' I looked at him, tried to smile cheerfully, to avoid transmitting any of the thoughts I'd been torturing myself with since I'd seen him holding Martha's hand as the bus left for the birthday party he wasn't invited to.

'What's up, cutie?' I asked.

'Don't worry, ma, I didn't want to go anyway.'

As soon as Mariano woke up, I was going to ask him to move us. The three of us, far away. I'd stayed up all night thinking about how to protect my son from the mistreatment he was receiving. He wouldn't let me see his pain, maybe didn't even allow himself to feel it, in order to protect me. But I knew the pain was there inside him even if he'd transformed it into something else. How much damage can be caused by suppressed sadness? So much damage. A silent, clandestine pain cuts deeper than one you can openly express.

That's why, after an entire night without so much as closing my eyes, weighing all the possible options, I concluded that nothing would change anytime soon, not even if we waited patiently like Mariano said we should. 'They'll get over it… Or not…' Martha had said outside the school. But I wasn't willing to let my son receive a new wound every day. The people around us weren't going to change. Their prejudices, hypocrisy, the need to punish him as a way of punishing me, would continue interfering with our lives. But we could change, start over, in a different house – it could even have a climbing rose if Mariano considered it important. A house in any other city, province, or country, just someplace where they didn't know our past, where none of Federico's classmates – or their parents – would have to decide if they were on our side or on the side of Juan's family. I didn't understand how this senseless divide had even been created. Why did anyone have to choose? Couldn't we all be on the same side, the side of the victims, the tragedy, the fatality? No, we couldn't. I wasn't allowed.

And my son had been dragged into it right along with me.

It was Saturday, so I waited for Mariano to wake up before leaving the bedroom. I was nervous, I couldn't go down to have breakfast in the kitchen and risk him leaving the house without saying goodbye, without giving me the opportunity to propose this solution I'd come up with. I knew it wasn't going to be easy, that he wasn't going to like the idea at first. But I was confident that, if he gave me the chance to explain, Mariano could be convinced that this was our best option. I laid out my entire plan as soon as he opened his eyes. 'You're crazy...' was the first thing he said. 'That would be admitting they're right, Marilé, that our son deserves to be left out.' Mariano looked at me and shook his head. 'You're crazy,' he said again, and then he hopped out of bed. He got dressed quickly, not because he had somewhere to be but because he wanted to get out of the bedroom before me. He didn't say it but it was clear by his body language, the agitation of someone putting up with an intolerable situation. He put his wallet in his pocket, picked up a light jacket and walked to the door. Before leaving he said: 'No, Marilé, I'm not going to allow it.' He was almost out of the room when I shouted at him in a harsh voice that I didn't recognize: 'But you are going to allow your son to be the only one not invited to a birthday party?' Mariano stopped, more surprised by my tone than by what I'd said. He came back into the bedroom and asked: 'Do you want the boy to hear you?' It was more a warning than a question. Then he closed the door and said: 'Time will fix things. It won't be like this the rest of our lives.' 'But it will be like this for a long time,' I replied. 'A long time that can do a lot of damage to Federico.' 'He's going to have to grow up, Marilé, he's going to have to be strong.' 'Why? It's not fair.' 'Because one of his friends died, the family is devastated... and because his mother is the one responsible for all that. That's what his luck has dealt him. He'll get through it, I have faith in him.'

He said it. My husband finally said what everyone else was saying: that I was guilty. Even though he'd been careful to use the word 'responsible' and not 'guilty'. My whole body was shaking. I wanted to say so many things but the words dissolved in my mind. All I could say was: 'They're never going to forgive me, are they?' 'I don't know,' Mariano said. 'I don't know how they're going to treat you but they'll eventually stop taking it out on Federico, I'm sure of that.' We looked at each other for a few moments in silence, trying to process what had been said, as well as what had gone unsaid. When I felt ready, I asked: 'So how am I meant to carry on living in such a hostile environment?' Mariano sighed, flapped his hands as he searched for the right words and then said: 'You're going to have to grow up too.' With a sob clenched between my jaws, I said again: 'I want us to move, Mariano, to start a new life somewhere else. Give me that chance.' And when I said 'give me that chance', I could no longer hold back the tears that came streaming down my face. No sobs, no blubbering, only tears. Mariano looked at me, this time not scornfully but with genuine pity, maybe even genuine sadness. 'Marilé, I work here. I'm the owner of a clinic that has been in this town since before you and I were born, a clinic that has become successful thanks to the hard work of my father first and now me. Do you know everything my family has sacrificed to make the clinic what it is today? Do you really think I can just throw all that out the window and start over somewhere else from scratch, as if I didn't come from somewhere, as if I had nothing? You can't ask that of me.' 'It's not for me, it's for Federico.' 'No, it's not for Federico, don't kid yourself. It's for you, Marilé.

141

Federico can handle it, Federico is strong. I'm going to teach him to become even stronger. You're the one who can't handle it, who will never be able to handle it, no matter how hard you try.' His words were an indictment. It didn't matter what I did, how much of an effort I made, I simply wasn't strong enough. I don't know where I found the nerve to keep pushing the issue: 'Well if you don't throw the clinic out the window, you're going to throw your family out the window, Mariano.' 'What family, Marilé?' I didn't need to say 'ours;' he knew perfectly well that I was talking about the three of us. I didn't respond because I understood what Mariano was trying to say with that question: 'What family?' He was saying we weren't 'the three of us' any more. I felt dizzy, trying to process what it meant if we were not a team, if there was no longer a collective noun that connected us, named us as one unit. No more 'family'. From now on it would be Mariano and Federico or Federico and I. 'So what do we do?' I asked. 'I don't know what you're going to do. Federico and I are going to keep doing the same thing we've been doing up to now, whether it hurts or not, the same thing.' For the first time since the accident I felt an emotion that superseded my sadness. It sat heavily on my chest, enraged, pushing my pain to the periphery. Was it hatred? I don't know, I prefer not to give it a name. How could Mariano exile me from that nucleus that was our family, the three of us, how dare he try to leave me out of their lives? I wouldn't allow it. 'Then Federico and I are leaving!' I shouted and I held Mariano's gaze. He shook his head, calmly, like someone who has everything figured out, and then he said: 'I'm not leaving and neither is Federico. You're not going to take away what we have. My father's clinic is going to be mine one day, and then someday it'll be Federico's. It represents a generational effort. You're not going to take away what is ours.' 'He's a six-year-old boy, what does he care about a clinic? We have to take care of him now, not after you die. The clinic will always belong to you, it doesn't matter where we live.' Mariano leaned over me, so furious that for a second I thought he was going to slap me. He waved his hands several times in the air, trying to control himself, trying to decide whether to do it or not. Then he clenched his fists and finally said, 'You think going off somewhere by yourself with him constitutes taking care of him? Pulling him out of his school? Moving him away from his grandparents, his family, his friends? Tell me, Marilé, what are you going to live on?' Mariano spat his questions and glared at me with his teeth barred, his eyes blazing. He rubbed his face and then placed his palms over his mouth, as if he were deciding whether to keep talking or not. But finally his anger won out and he went on: 'Do you have any idea how fast I could get a judge to take custody from you and give Federico right back to me? You killed a kid. He died because of your negligence. Are you ever going to understand that? I assure you that any judge who has to decide where Federico lives is going to understand it, and if not, I'll make them understand.' His words were worse than the slap he'd held back. 'Federico and I are staying. You can do whatever you want. Or whatever you're capable of.' He opened the bedroom door to leave again, so I placed my hand on the doorframe to stop him. 'Are you telling me to go?' I asked. Mariano stood there without saying a word. 'You're telling me to go,' I repeated, this time not a question but a statement. Mariano pushed my arm out of the way but he didn't leave the room. 'I'm telling you that Federico and I are strong enough to put up with this as long as it lasts. If you're strong enough too, stay, if not, do what you have to do.' 'I'm his mother,' I said in a final attempt to reclaim my rightful position. 'There are many kinds of mothers. Some mothers, when they see that they're ruining their child's life, will find a way to stop.'

And then finally, after saying that, he left.

I didn't immediately understand everything Mariano had said to me, but his words would stay with me forever like a script I'd memorized. By heart, as they say, and I think the metaphor applies because his words were branded on my heart, engraved there. Looking back, I'm not sure I was willing to hear everything he'd said. His sentences tumbled around in my head, literally, word for word, but the meaning came only in flashes, like a lightbulb flickering out. It must have been my way of protecting myself: if I'd fully comprehended his intention I might've fallen down dead right then and there. It seemed wiser to let myself play dumb. It was true that if we left, Federico would have a life very different to the one we'd dreamed of for him. But if we stayed, people would continue to make my son pay for what I'd done, keeping him from living the full life he deserved.

I was trapped, I knew that one way or another, no matter what I chose, it was a losing game.

I went out for a walk, wandering aimlessly for a while until I found myself on the pedestrian bridge that crossed over the Turdera train station, some twenty blocks from my house. I heard the train whistle and I froze. It was a different train, a different whistle, and I wasn't inside a car waiting for the barrier arm to raise with two kids singing 'Incy Wincy Spider' in the back seat. But for the entire time it took the train to enter the station, the passengers to get off, new ones to get on, and the train to depart, my blood remained frozen in my veins. I couldn't think about anything until the train pulled away and I could no longer see or hear it. I stood there, my elbows on the bridge railing, looking down at the empty platform, Mariano's words drifting through my head. Until finally, who knows why, his voice stopped and I grasped the meaning behind the words he'd said to me that morning: Federico would only win back everyone's respect and affection if I disappeared from his life. I was singularly responsible for the mistreatment he received. The others were just there to point it out. Confirming something I'd always known: I would never be a good mother, I wasn't programmed that way, I didn't know how to be one, there was something wrong with me. I was the one who crossed the tracks with the arm down. I was the one driving when the car stalled and wouldn't start back up. I was the one to blame for Juan's death. I was the one hated by the entire town. Only me. But that hatred ran downhill onto Federico. My son, who, unlike everyone else, was still on my side. He tried to protect me, called me 'Ma' and lied to me as best he could so that I wouldn't suffer any more than I was already suffering. That's too much to ask of a six-year-old child. Federico couldn't carry my weight any longer, he shouldn't have to. If I wasn't there, if I'd died along with Juan that day, for example, Federico would've been showered with love, pity, condolences. He would've been devastated over my death but it would not have been a secret pain, not something he had to hide. He could've expressed his grief, cried it all out, and then, little by little, begun to heal until his dead mother was nothing but a sad, distant memory, an occasional sense of nostalgia, a grave he could bring flowers to on the anniversary of the tragedy, a framed photograph collecting dust in the house we'd once shared.

But I hadn't died that day along with Juan. I was here. Still. On a bridge a few blocks from our house watching the trains come and go without killing anyone. How could I make myself disappear so that my son could have his life back? My first thought was suicide. I could've done it right then and there. Throw myself under the next train. But suicide is a very particular kind of death that has repercussions for the ones left behind. It's a death dedicated to them – even if it wasn't meant to be – that makes them feel responsible for not having realized what was about to happen, for not having done anything to stop it. I knew that Federico, at age six, would feel responsible for my suicide. So I discarded the idea of taking my own life. I was trembling from head to toe. If I didn't kill myself, what could I do? I started walking back the way I'd come. Shaking, walking, and thinking. Thoughts raced through my mind much faster than normal. They came in images: Federico's face, Mariano's, the climbing rose, my crushed car, the train, the school, Juan kicking and screaming, the hospital, Federico looking for Juan in the sky, a tiny grave, my face, the train, all flashing past over and over in the same order, or in any order.

Stopped on a street corner, I realized that suicide didn't only feel wrong because of the damage it would do to Federico, but for reasons that had more to do with me. Before, on the Turdera bridge, when I'd accepted that Mariano would never leave this place and these people, suicide had felt like the best option. To free my son from his mother, from what his mother meant to everyone around him, even his father. I'd finally have the death that everyone thought I deserved. There, on the bridge, I'd turned the idea over in my mind, I'd wanted it. And the fact that I wanted it made it wrong. Killing myself might free him of me, but I'd also be freeing myself. It would put an end to my pain, it would be over. Only mine. My pain would end the day I pulled the trigger, filled my mouth with pills, stuck my head in the oven and turned on the gas. Or threw myself under a train. That day, finally, I'd be free. No more pain. A moral ending like in some old-fashioned novel: the woman finally comprehends the gravity of her actions and receives the punishment she deserves; she pays for murder with her own death. *Lex talionus*: an eye for an eye.

But Talion's law didn't apply here. I'd never experience the amount of pain I'd caused even if they tied me to the tracks and let the train run me over. It would never be enough. It would never be fair. I might be able to escape my own suffering but Federico would still suffer, in a different way. So, if ending my life wasn't the solution, what could I do to help my son? How could I free him from the pain I'd caused him? How could I disappear from his life forever without killing myself? How far will a mother go to spare her child pain? Something she never thought herself capable of that suddenly seems like a law of nature, the only possible option? If that limit isn't death, what is it? Going, leaving him, abandoning him and never seeing him again. A pain worse than death that never goes away, even grows larger, taking on unthinkable, unfathomable dimensions. Imagining my son growing up, his hair getting darker, his voice deeper, his little boy's face turning into a man's, and not being there. To be aware that it's happening, inevitably, and not being able to witness it. To have no idea what he's studying in school, what profession he chooses, who he falls in love with, decides to walk through life with, to have children with, never meeting those kids who are not your grandchildren. My grandchildren. To know he's somewhere out there walking around, going to sleep, crying, laughing, dreaming, suffering, having fun, and never being there.

Not being there, that was the kind of suffering I deserved. To keep on living, without him. Much worse than suicide, without a doubt. An endless, bottomless pain. The agony of never being able to hug him again. I started crying, inconsolably, harder than I'd ever cried, sadness pouring from my body, emptying out of me. I'd have to rip myself in two, separate the person I was from the one I'd become. Neither Juan's death nor the mistreatment my son received afterward had caused me as much agony as the thought of leaving and never seeing my son again. To go on living, split in half, divided, broken. Submerged in that deep sadness, I knew what I had to do: to leave and never come back, to never see Federico again. He would suffer the pain of abandonment but that was repairable, collateral damage, the gentlest option I could choose for him. It was much better than that secret suffering he'd otherwise have to endure forever. The abandonment would leave wounds. But once they'd healed, even if the scars might remain imprinted on his skin, my son would be able to find his path, to find love, a family. Everything I'd never have again. Because, unlike with suicide, mine would be a living death.

To leave and yet go on living: no punishment could be worse.

I went back to the house. Mariano and Federico weren't there, they must've gone to the club, or to visit friends. Or Martha. It was better this way, if they were home I might not have been able to do it. His presence would have changed everything. I would've had to wait for a better time and any delay in a decision like that would've allowed doubts to creep in. And I needed to act without hesitation. They weren't there, so I was able to go through with it. I put a few things in a small suitcase. I grabbed my passport, credit cards, and two thousand dollars from Mariano's safe in the closet, which would allow me to take my first steps away from home.

I packed the three photos of Federico that I still carry with me to this day.

And I left.

I got to Ezeiza without any destination in mind. It didn't matter as long as it was somewhere far away. I found a flight that left in an hour for Miami and there were still some seats available. I had a visa to get into the United States, we'd got it for me after getting married but before Federico was born. Mariano had a convention for work near San Francisco, a few days, less than a week, and I went with him. I never used it again. I wonder now if that visa, which I only used for three days, hadn't been obtained – in one of those twists of fate we only see after the fact – so that the day I left I could take that plane to Miami and nowhere else, to be seated three rows behind Robert and nowhere else.

I was in a state of shock. That dazed woman going through the motions was the person I'd now become. Taking the steps necessary to purchase the ticket and complete check-in, get as far away from her son as possible, as quickly as possible. Without thinking, without crying. Without doing anything besides what it took to leave before she had time to regret it.

In the line to check my bags I realized I should've picked a different destination. With just a quick look around I saw a few familiar faces. I couldn't quite place them, I didn't know their names, but they were faces I'd seen before, around the neighbourhood or at school. I put on my sunglasses, lowered my head, kept my eyes fixed on my suitcase. Even if I didn't know who they were, they'd surely know who I was: the woman who crossed the train tracks when the barrier was down and killed a little boy. A woman who would've gone completely unnoticed if she hadn't become a sad celebrity after that incident. A horrible woman, as the pharmacist in Temperley said to me a few days before I started writing this text. A woman damaged, as Robert said. It was too late to change the destination now but as soon as I got to Miami I'd find a cheap flight, to any other city in the United States, one I'd never even heard of if possible, where it would be harder to run into anyone who knew me. A city that by chance ended up being Boston.

I met Robert on the plane after he changed seats with the woman next to me. A little luck changed my fate. If I'd never met him, I might have just let myself die as soon as I reached Miami, or whatever unknown city I ended up in. Not by suicide, just letting my life slip away, little by little, like the thread of smoke from a cigarette as it turns to ash, without doing anything to stop it. But there, on that plane, was Robert, three rows in front of me, in the emergency exit row. The woman next to me was travelling with her son, who was seated somewhere else. She complained to the flight attendant, who told the woman to wait, to be patient, that they'd try to sort it out once all the passengers had boarded the plane. But the woman would not be patient and instead tried to solve the problem herself by speaking directly to the person seated beside her son, but the man said no, that he could only sit in an aisle seat, he didn't want to swap it for a middle seat. I don't know why she didn't ask me. Maybe she didn't want her son to lose the window seat he'd been assigned. Maybe it was just the look on my face that intimidated her. Or maybe she did ask me but I didn't hear her. I had my eyes fixed on the seatback in front of me, only seeing things around me out of the corner of my eye, like a horse with blinkers on so they don't get spooked. But even if I wasn't paying much attention, I understood what was happening. The woman was going up and down the aisle, blocking people's way as they tried to board. The flight attendant asked her several times to sit and wait, but the woman would just step out of the way for a minute and then wander back into the aisle. Until Robert, who was six feet six inches tall, gave his seat – on the bulkhead, the most comfortable seat in economy, which he'd surely booked in advance – to the passenger seated beside the boy. So the mother moved into the man's seat and Robert came to sit in the middle seat beside me.

I had to stand up so he could get by. He apologized in English and in Spanish as he stuffed his large body into that small space that was now his spot on the plane. I caught a whiff of a cologne that I recognized from somewhere, but it was not a cologne Mariano had ever used, something sweeter and softer than the ones worn by the person who had been my husband until that morning, just a few hours prior. I searched my memory for that smell but I couldn't place it. The feeling it produced in me was as if my father had worn it. Except my father had never worn cologne. Maybe it was an aftershave. Today I think it might have been the same cologne Maplethorpe wore; I'm not sure, all I know is that, in the state I was in, that smell made me feel like I could trust him. In a moment in which no other auditory, visual, or tactile sensation could reach me, Robert's cologne managed to breach the shield I'd put up. It told me that this man now sitting beside me wore the same cologne as someone I trusted. The plane took off and there was no window near enough for me to take one last glimpse of this place I knew I wouldn't be seeing again for a long time. I'll never see this place again, I thought. But I was wrong, because here I am.

I didn't cry on the flight, but I shook the whole way. From take-off to landing, I trembled from head to toe. Sometimes it was a gentle quiver, almost imperceptible. Sometimes it was a violent jolting. The passenger in front of me even turned around to complain that I'd kicked their seat. Robert gave me a wink to let me know he was on my side and not the side of the man who was annoyed by my movements. During dinner service I didn't even open my tray table and firmly shook my head at everything the flight attendant offered. 'Maybe a glass of wine would help settle your nerves. Un poco de vino?' Robert said soothingly, in an accent that sounded British to my ears. I smiled. I don't know where I found the strength to smile at him. He was a warm man, trustworthy, someone who'd forgone personal comfort so that a woman he didn't know could travel beside her son. And who wore a cologne that somehow managed to penetrate the wall I'd built around myself so that nothing – no feeling, sensation, thought – could get through to me and make me feel pain, sadness, love, devastation, or anything. But that cologne and the feelings it evoked – although I wasn't able to connect it to any specific person – could. I smiled but I didn't answer. 'Do you have a fear of flying?' he asked me. 'No,' I answered. Without any further explanation, just no, and I kept on trembling. 'If you need anything, just let me know,' he said, and he didn't speak to me again for the rest of the flight.

But he was forced to speak to me when we landed and I refused to stand up. Almost all the passengers had already got off the plane and I was still sitting there, unable to move. He waited, patiently, until he must have concluded that if he didn't ask me to get up he'd be stuck there forever. So I finally stood up, collected my purse, and walked towards the exit, without saying anything, without smiling. He trailed behind me. And a little while after walking off the plane and down the jetway, on one of those long hallways leading who knows where, I fainted. I don't know exactly what happened after that, but I came to in a room that looked like an infirmary. Robert was standing beside the doctor who was examining me. He said that my blood pressure had dropped, that it was no big deal, that everything was fine. The doctor nodded, as if Robert had repeated her diagnosis word for word. But once I'd recovered we were shown into a nearby office where some immigration agents started asking questions, most of which I was unable to answer. The most important one, the address of the place I'd be staying during my visit to the United States. The third time they asked the question without my answering, Robert answered for me: 'She's going to stay at my house, in Boston, as my guest.' Then they asked him several questions too quickly and in too strong of an accent for me to follow. I caught some of his answers: his name, Robert Lohan, that he was a school principal, that he didn't have a family, that he lived in Boston. They took our passports and left. We waited for a long time. When they came back they started saying things to Robert that I didn't understand, but every once in a while I thought I caught the word Vietnam. It was the only time during the exhaustive interrogation that I thought I perceived a certain tension in Robert's voice. Finally, they let us go. We walked silently down another one of those endless airport hallways. And only once we were far enough away from the place we'd been interrogated, Robert asked me to sit for a moment and then he sat down beside me. He spoke to me in Spanish, a stumbling and stuttering Spanish that left out many words and mispronounced all the rest. Trying to speak my language was his way of showing that he wanted to help: 'I don't know who you are, I don't know why you're shaking so much, but if you don't have anywhere to go, you can come to my house. I live in Boston, and I have a room I rent to students sometimes. It's empty now and you can use it until you stop shaking and you figure out where you want to go.' 'I don't know where I want to go,' I said. 'I can see that, that's why I'm offering to let you come to my house and take some time to think about it.' He smiled at me. I smiled back. What else could I do.

I let myself be swept along. By that time, Robert had missed his connection to Boston, so we went to book my ticket and to rebook his for the same flight. 'What's your name? Blanche DuBois?' he said to me as we were waiting. 'Sorry, you said it in the infirmary but you seem like you could be a Blanche.' I just stared. 'Blanche DuBois,' he said again. I didn't understand. 'I've always relied on the kindness of strangers,' he said. I still didn't get it. 'That's what Blanche DuBois says. Sorry, it's a Tennessee Williams character. You remind me of her.' 'It's true, you're being very kind, yes,' I said and I thought that maybe it had been his kindness and not his cologne that had penetrated the shield I'd put up around myself. 'You're very kind,' I said again. 'I'm not talking about me, I'm talking about you,' he said. 'Every time I read or see *A Streetcar Named Desire* in the theatre, when Blanche says those lines, I think that a person who has to rely on the kindness of strangers must be all alone in the world. Even if they're surrounded by people. If someone has to rely on the kindness of strangers it's because the people around them aren't people they can count on.' His words described me so perfectly that I shuddered. I kept the conversation going as I attempted to control my shaking: 'Like the woman you gave your seat to on the plane, for example,' I said. But Robert wouldn't let me change the subject. 'You… María? Your name's María?' 'María,' I confirmed. 'Do you rely on the kindness of strangers because you don't have anyone you can count on? I don't know anything about your past, your childhood, your family; anything up to the moment we met on the plane, but when I saw you yesterday, and today, here, I thought, that woman seems utterly alone.' I started to cry. Robert handed me his handkerchief, he held it out and waited for me to decide if I would accept it or not. And then he let me cry. Without asking, without saying any words of consolation. Just cry. The situation was highly unusual: I'd left my country, abandoned my son, got on the first available plane, and I now found myself crying beside a man who didn't know me or understand the reasons for my tears but who was a kind stranger I could rely on. Not only that, I was going to Boston, a city totally foreign to me, with a man I knew nothing about besides his name and his cologne, because he seemed kind and he offered to rent me a room in his house. Robert Lohan, someone who could've been a serial killer instead of a kind stranger to my Blanche DuBois.

But what could a serial killer do to me that would be worse than what I'd done to myself by abandoning my son?

The early days of my life in Boston were spent in my room at Robert's. It was separated from the rest of the house by a courtyard and we hardly ever saw each other. He would drop by from time to time to ask if I needed anything. But he was careful not to intrude, not to go beyond the limits of what he sensed I could tolerate. One day he brought me a Spanish edition of *A Streetcar Named Desire*. 'I found it in a second-hand bookshop; I saw that it was in Spanish and I said to myself that it was for you.' I put the book on my night table and only picked it up a few days later. I finished it in a day and returned it. He told me to keep it, that it had been a gift, that he preferred to read Tennessee Williams in English. 'Thank you,' I said and I was about to go back to my room with the book but something made me turn around and say to him: 'Even though I have relied on the kindness of strangers, like Blanche DuBois, I'm nothing like her. And her story is nothing like mine.' 'I didn't give you the book because I thought you were just like Blanche. But I think we all have a little of Blanche in us, me included. That's the way it always is with classic characters, there's something everyone can identify with, some point, some gesture that lets us connect with them. Or at least put ourselves in their position.' Robert took the book and flipped through it, as if he were looking for some specific scene, then he read some lines to himself and closed it. 'But beyond any points of overlap, did you like the book?' he asked. 'Yes, I liked it a lot,' I answered. 'I'll keep trying, then,' said Robert.

A few days later he brought me *The Woman Destroyed*, by Simone de Beauvoir. I knew immediately that I wouldn't leave that book sitting on my night table. I was disturbed by the title. I read it that very afternoon. I cried. When I got to the end, I cried harder than I'd cried in front of Robert at the airport, when he'd handed me the handkerchief that I never returned. The book had jarred something loose and unleashed all the tears I'd been holding in since well before the day I ran away. When I finally collected myself, I went to return the book. This book wasn't a gift, like the other one had been: his name was written on the first page, Robert Lohan, the way people write their names in books when they expect them to be returned. He had to offer me another handkerchief. 'Number two,' he said. I explained that in my country we considered it bad luck to return a handkerchief. 'Your country is a very unusual place,' he said. 'Do you know it well?' 'No, very little. I spent a week in Chile for work and only two days in Buenos Aires, I just had to see that city I'd heard so much about. And to meet you on that plane,' he said, smiling shyly. 'And why do you think it so unusual if you don't know it very well?' 'Because the people there never return handker-chiefs!' he replied and laughed. I laughed too, I couldn't remember the last time I'd laughed. I tried to search my memory, but I stopped myself immediately, knowing that when I found it, Federico would be there. I wasn't yet prepared for that encounter, so I stopped diving down into my memory and resurfaced instead. 'Thanks for the book,' I said. And then, almost immediately: 'A man didn't leave me for another woman.' Robert grinned. 'But did you like the book?' 'Very much,' I answered. 'Even though I'm not that woman.' 'The same mistake again. I didn't say you were,' Robert clarified, 'I knew the book would make you cry. And I thought crying might provide some relief, a release of whatever you've been holding in, trembling over.' 'How do you know I cried when I read it?' 'Because of your eyes, they're still damp, and red. And because I cried when I read it.' He smiled and I smiled. 'I did cry,' I confessed, 'you're right about that.' I was about to go back to my room but he stopped me. 'Wait a second, I have another book for you; if you'll give me a minute I'll get it now.' He went to his bookshelf and returned with a book in his hand. He flipped until he got to a specific page and he folded the corner down. 'Alice Munro,' he said. 'Short stories, all very good, but start with the one I've marked, "The Children Stay".' I took the book, '"The Children Stay",' I repeated, thanked him, and left.

I started reading it at two o'clock in the morning. An hour later I knocked on Robert's door. I was crying inconsolably but this time he didn't have to lend me a handkerchief because I was carrying one of the ones he'd already lent me. And I was angry. 'You have no right to do this to me,' I said enraged. Robert didn't respond. 'Who do you think you are?' I shouted. Robert still didn't say anything. 'And who does this Alice Munro think she is?' I asked as I threw the book on the floor, as if ridding myself of something disgusting. Robert bent down to pick it up – I think it pained him to see it mistreated, its spine bent – he smoothed the pages a little and said: 'Munro is a great writer.' And then he stood there silently staring at me, waiting for me to calm down. He gave me my time, unhurriedly, without complaint. Gradually my breath slowed, my heart stopped pounding in my chest. I didn't apologize. I arrogantly demanded: 'Does that woman know what she's talking about or is she lying?' 'Alice Munro?' 'Yes.' 'She lies truthfully, like any good writer,' Robert answered, 'and if she lies truthfully, it's because she knows what she's talking about.' Then, as if reciting from memory, I began to list the questions that I'd asked myself while reading Alice Munro's story, questions posed in her words. 'Is it true that the pain will become chronic? Is it true that it will be permanent but not constant, that I won't die from the pain? Is it true that someday I won't feel it every minute, even though I won't spend many days without it?' I asked these questions through sobs that I didn't even try to suppress because it would've been futile. It was impossible to separate those tears from the questions the story had brought to the surface. Robert was silent for a moment and then finally said: 'That's the way it is with some kinds of pain. I don't know what kind yours is.' 'I left my son, but not for a man,' I answered. 'I see that you're alone, utterly alone.' I frowned, annoyed at hearing my loneliness described so brutally. So I tried to be brutal back: 'And you, why are you so alone? What are you hiding? Why did the officers who questioned us in Miami mention Vietnam so many times?' That last question seemed to ruffle Robert's cool exterior. 'If you want to come in, I'll tell you about it,' he said. I went inside and we sat in the chairs in front of the bookshelves. 'My brother died in Vietnam. I didn't go, I was enrolled in college and managed to use that to keep from enlisting. I didn't agree with the war. My parents did, my brother made them proud. I didn't. In spite of my parents and in spite of his own wishes, I tried to convince my brother not to go. But he had to, and he wanted to. So he went. He wrote frequently at first, he was euphoric. Then he became less and less communicative. In the end, my brother was only writing to me, not my parents, and his letters were only a paragraph or two at most. I memorized the last letter I received from him like a poem after reading it so many times.

I killed a lot of people today,

I don't know how many,

I don't know who,
I wouldn't recognize their faces,
but I know I killed them.
It wasn't the first time.
But today I knew it.
Why?
What for?

I didn't get any more letters from him. Only the official communication that he'd been killed in combat. My parents couldn't handle the news. They both died not long after that. One after the other. And I joined any anti-war group I could find. For a while I was going every afternoon to protest in front of the White House, asking the president to stop the war. There were more and more of us. I got arrested for protesting several times. Sometimes those arrests pop up on the computers at the airport. But once they see the reasons for the arrests they're usually more embarrassed than I am. Vietnam syndrome, no one wants to remember it. And they always let me go without asking too many more questions.' Robert paused, stared at me for a moment, and then said: 'Do you want to tell me about yourself?' I sighed, I wasn't sure that I wanted to, but I felt that Robert deserved an explanation. 'I didn't leave my son because of a man like the character in the Alice Munro story, even though I feel a similar pain,' I said. And then I added: 'I left to protect him from me.' 'What harm could you do to your son that you have to protect him from?' 'It's a long story,' I answered, 'and it's late.' I stood up. Robert stood up after me and said: 'Whenever you want, whenever you're ready, I'll be here to listen to your story.' 'I've always relied on the kindness of strangers,' I said and for the first time I smiled at him before he smiled at me. Robert returned my smile as he walked me to the door and I left.

A few days passed. Robert didn't come by my room

to lend me any books. I didn't go near his part of the house. I was trying to gather the courage to tell him about my past and he was giving me the time to do it. Until finally one afternoon, I don't know how many days later, I knocked on his door and asked: 'Do you really want to hear my story?' 'I want to hear it, yes, of course I do.' I went inside, Robert followed me. We sat in the same chairs as before, in front of the bookshelves. I told him everything, adding details that I hadn't even been aware of before. I think I told my story that way, so precisely, because in doing so I was telling myself my story for the first time: my parents, the brother I never knew, the bats, the pull of the abyss, the railway crossing, my son, Mariano, the train, a dead child, being hated by everyone around me, Martha, Saint Peter's School, my house with the climbing rose, the Turdera bridge, my son's voice calling my name, his hand, his six-year-old skin. 'What I miss most about him is his skin, touching his soft warm hand as we walked down the street together.' I looked at Robert and asked: 'Now do you know who I am?' 'Yes, I think I do: a woman damaged,' Robert answered. 'Not a woman destroyed, like in Simone de Beauvoir's book, just a woman damaged.' 'And is that better or worse?' I asked. 'It's much better,' said Robert. 'Why?' 'Because damage can be repaired, wounds sewn up, scars healed. Something that's broken is harder to repair, it's often better to just replace it. But something that's simply damaged can be fixed. There's hope that it can be restored, I'm not saying always back to its original state, but good enough to keep going. Maybe slower, weaker, but still going. My brother couldn't have been repaired. I knew it when I read his last letter. They'd broken him. But maybe you can. I don't know, I don't know you well enough. What happened, the events in themselves, can't be fixed. They've already happened, there's no changing them. They will always be there. In your past. But today, tomorrow, next year, all depend on how you live and what you do as you move on. The damage is done, the pain is there, but the paths you choose will determine what's to come. You can't erase the pain, but you can turn it into something you're able to tolerate a little more every day, that's always with you but that allows you to carry on. Even if you don't spend many days without it, like Alice Munro says, one morning you might be able to leave the house and take a walk without it. One day you may even feel ready to return to the place you left…' Robert would've kept going but I interrupted him: 'I left my son to protect him, and it's for him that I can never go back. He's not safe with me there. And I don't think anything can repair the loss of a child.' 'You'll have to wait and see,' Robert answered, 'you'll have to wait and see.' Then he stood up and came back with two glasses of wine. 'A woman damaged. I suspected that's what you were, but I thought you were a woman who'd been damaged for a long time, not just now but injury upon injury, pain on pain, until you couldn't take it any more.' I started trembling again like I had on the flight. The wine sloshed in the glass. Robert took it and set it on the table. Then he held my hand and told me I could stay at his house that night if I didn't want to be alone. 'Don't misunderstand me, I'm not making an indecent proposal, I just think you might sleep better here.' He gave me his room and he took the couch. I woke up in the middle of the night and Robert was sitting at the end of the bed. 'You were dreaming, screaming in your sleep, I didn't want to wake you up, sorry.' 'What was I saying?' 'You were shouting a name: Juan.' 'The boy I killed.' 'The boy who died on the tracks,' said Robert, and he stood up. Before he left the room I asked him: 'Could you hold my hand until I fall asleep?' He didn't respond, he just sat back down on the bed, right beside me, and he placed my hand between his. I closed my eyes and let myself be led by the hand back into sleep.

We didn't hug until several months later. I'd been living in Boston for over a year, taking translation jobs that Robert asked me to do for him, more as a way to help me than because he really needed it, I suspect. Or because they were texts he wanted me to read. One night he came to my room to bring me a story that, according to him, he needed to use with some students. The story was 'Wakefield', by Nathaniel Hawthorne. Before handing it to me, he said: 'I already know that the main character is nothing like you, so you don't have to clarify that after you read it. I wasn't looking for coincidences. But I think the end is interesting. A man who leaves his family for many years, goes to live in a house very close by but no one knows where he is all that time, until one day he goes back.' 'Was he a murderer?' 'No, he wasn't a murderer,' Robert answered, 'but I don't think you fall into that category either, despite the fact that a boy was run over by a train. Sometimes I wonder if my brother would fall into that category. He killed people. He'd wanted to enlist in that war. But he only knew what it meant to kill someone after he realized he'd been deceived. Could he have done anything different? I don't know, I'll never know.' I felt like Robert needed something from me after having given so much. 'Do you want to come in?' I asked. 'I have enough wine for two half glasses.' 'That's better than nothing,' he replied and came in. He talked all night about his brother, his parents. The difficulties he'd had in maintaining stable relationships with the few women he'd fallen in love with. About how he was so used to living alone. 'Until you got here,' he said. 'Now I'm used to having you around to share a book or a glass of wine with from time to time. You're good for me,' he said, and that must've been one of the nicest things anyone had ever said to me. 'You're good for me,' he repeated and I stood up and hugged him. It was an impulse, the first impulse I'd had in a long time. Ever since I'd left my country, since I'd abandoned my son, every move I'd made was calculated, I couldn't take a single step without carefully considering it first, couldn't make myself a meal without going back and forth about what to eat, couldn't take a shower without deliberating over when it would be best to take it. But that night I simply stood up and hugged Robert without any thoughts getting in the way of the impulse and the action. And he let me hug him.

Over time we realized that neither one of us could live without the other one, or that living without the other one made things much harder for both of us. We started spending all our time together. Sometimes in his part of the house. Sometimes in my room. The first kiss didn't come until several months after that. As if it were something we'd simply overlooked. Holding hands was enough, hugging occasionally. But, fundamentally, being able to count on each other. Kissing, physicality, helped us become even closer still. But that came later, in due time. If it had come too soon we wouldn't have been ready, one of us might have rejected it. We achieved a kind of communion that one day required kissing and physicality; if it had been the other way around it might not have worked.

Robert's lips and his body completed me, and even though I never stopped being a woman damaged, he was able to repair me, to a point. 'Total repair will depend on you, there are some spots I can't reach, someday you'll have to decide if you want to keep living the years you have left this way or if there's something different you want to do. I know what I'd like you to do, but it's your decision. It will always be your decision.' And Robert waited until he knew that he couldn't wait any more, because he was dying. Convinced that without his help I might never take that step I still had yet to take – to see my son again, even if just once. Robert didn't want to leave everything up to fate, so he took action. Fate wanted Saint Peter's to apply to become an affiliated school, but Robert did everything else. I now suspect Robert might even have offered to evaluate Saint Peter's and that my being sent to do the evaluation was less of a coincidence than I'd supposed. I'll never know for sure. I can't ask Robert, he's not here. Yet I feel like I know him better and better every day. And it makes me smile to think that despite being dead he's still with me, he continues to do things for me, not from a greater beyond that I don't believe in, but things he did for me here, in this world, before he left it, and I'm seeing them only now.

And that's how I ended up back here in this place I left twenty years ago. Thanks to the kindness of strangers. Thanks to my luck, not the kind of luck my mother said I had, but a little luck. Maybe a bunch of little luck added up. Thanks to my father who reassured me that the bats wouldn't get tangled in my hair like my mother feared. Thanks to Maplethorpe who told me: 'You have to be strong.'

Thanks to Robert.

And thanks to my son, who no longer has soft six-year-old skin, but who had the courage to confront the mother who abandoned him.

To confront me.

I print the text as soon as I'm finished. It's Sunday night and I want to give it to my son tomorrow, to place it in his hands, when I go back to Saint Peter's for the last time to meet with Mr Galván and say goodbye. The printer they've set up in the office works fine, but the letters fade from black to grey as the pages pile up and I'm afraid the ink might run out before getting to the end. Some of the sheets slip out of the printer tray and get mixed up so I have to skim them to put them back in order. I read random words, the end of one sentence and the beginning of another: Ezeiza, boy, Wakefield, wine, trust, train. Juan. The printer gets through the text, in spite of the ink cartridge, and I look to the last lines. In shades of grey but clearly legible, I read: 'To confront me.'

I straighten the pages, tapping them on one side and then the other until they've formed a neat pile. I put them in an envelope I find rummaging in the desk drawers. On the front I write my son's name: Federico Lauría. I turn it over to put my name on the back but I hesitate; I don't know whether to put Mary Lohan or Marilé Lauría. Or María Elena Pujol, my real name, the name my parents gave me when I was born. Finally I decide not to put anything, my son knows who wrote this text and I'll place it in his hands – even if I didn't he would still know – and so the sender's name is unnecessary. But I pull the text from the envelope and I write my name on the last page: María Elena Pujol. I know that Robert would understand. I know that my son needs to see that name. And so do I. Below I add my email address, just in case, after reading it, he has anything to say to me.

I'm about to seal the envelope but before doing so I realize there's something missing. I go to my room and rummage in my backpack. I take out the three photos of Federico that travelled beside Robert's. I lay them out on the bed, I look at them, try to pick one but I can't. I close my eyes. I choose one at random, the first one I touch. I open my eyes and look at it. It's an image of Federico at just over one year old. He's toddling towards the camera, holding out his arms. In reality he's not walking towards the person behind the lens, Mariano. He's walking on a slant towards me, even though I'm not in the frame. But I know I'm there. Because I was there, holding out my arms to make him feel safe, encouraging him to come to us. I go back to the desk and slip the photo inside the envelope, but first I give it a kiss, as if I were saying goodbye to it. I'm surprised at myself, I'm not the kind of person who kisses things, I don't say goodbye.

I set out for the school on foot. I forgot to tell Mr Galván not to pick me up this morning so I leave a few minutes early to avoid running into him. I want to take one last walk, alone. I wave goodbye to the doorman as I leave the building. He looks at me without saying anything. Now that he thinks the bat has flown away — if he in fact believed me — we have nothing to say to each other. I raise a hand in a weak wave and I leave the building.

Halfway there, on a whim, before I have time to think about it and change my mind, I turn right, walk three blocks, and find myself standing opposite the house where I used to live. I observe it from a distance. I'm not going to cross to the other side, but I want to see it. Even from where I am, I can see that the climbing rose is no longer there. I wonder if it simply died or if Martha decided to replace it with the unfamiliar plants I see there now. I also wonder if my son still lives with them, but I discard the idea almost immediately. If he got married, had a daughter, chose to do the opposite of what his father would've wanted him to professionally, and especially if my son is what he proved himself to be when he confronted me with his text, Federico must live somewhere else. He's surely trying to write his own story independently of the past, starting a new family, maybe without rejecting this one, but a family of his own. That's what I believe my son would have done, that's what I hope, but I don't know. The door opens and a young man walks out. It's not Federico. It's probably one of Martha's sons, though I don't recognize him from this distance. I might not even recognize him if he were standing right in front of me. He takes a few steps in my direction. I wonder if I should walk away or stand there pretending to look for something in my purse or at my phone, stalling for time until he gets to where I am, looks at me – or not – and keeps going. But instead the young man gets into a car and drives away. So I take a few steps closer, as if having successfully dodged one risk has given me the courage to take a better look around. I see a silhouette in the living room window, someone coming and going. I don't know who it is. Mariano? Martha? Does it matter? Standing there so close to this house that was once my home makes my mouth go dry. I swallow in an attempt to moisten it but my throat remains parched. My legs ache, my calves feel like they're full of shards. My body is uncomfortable here. I begin to shake, a controlled quivering that no one else would notice. But my discomfort goes beyond my dry throat, leg cramps and shaking. I'm uneasy standing here opposite this house again because it confirms in my mind that I was never happy there. And then I ask myself: was I ever happy? In that house with Mariano and Federico, or before with my parents in their little apartment with the terrace and the bats, or at school in my childhood innocence, in my young arrogance on that trip to Pinamar, was I happy? And after I left this house? It's hard to be happy after abandoning your child. I don't count the death of his friend as a permanent obstacle to happiness because that's a guilt of another order, I carry it with me, it weighs on me, returns as a constant regret, but it doesn't cancel out all possibility of happiness. Having left my son does. The time after my life here was a time of dormant emotions, of numbed feelings. As if I were some electronic device that needed 220 volts to function properly but they'd plugged me into 110. My relationship with Robert was loving and supportive. But happiness is something else entirely. When Robert handed me a glass of wine, put on a jazz album, sat down beside me with a book and held my hand, when we travelled together and found ourselves in some new and disturbingly beautiful landscape, when we went to the theatre and enjoyed an unforgettable show, when we slept with our arms around each other, I might have felt relief, calm, affection, consolation, even hope, but I could never say: I am happy. I've never been able to say that, not before, not after, not now. Maybe some people simply aren't wired for happiness. Some of us, when we feel joy circling close, fly into a state of panic. And we'll do whatever it takes to avoid it, to push it out of our path before it descends on us. Because we'd have no idea what to do with that happiness, how to make it fit inside our bodies so that we can continue moving forward. For some of us, unease, not happiness, is the only habitat in which we feel we can survive.

I stand there a little while longer, across from that house, and then I retrace my steps to my previous route. But when I get to the station I cross over to the Lauría Health and Wellness Clinic, which belonged to my father-in-law, which today must belong to Mariano and might become Federico's one day. The building has changed a lot. It's clear they've done well. It's been renovated to look very modern and they've expanded into the neighbouring properties; the ambulances parked outside the emergency room seem to be the latest models. People march constantly in and out. That's where they treated me after the incident at the railway crossing. Or the events at the railway crossing. I can never find the right word for what happened. I don't like saying 'the accident'. That makes it seem like something unavoidable, erases my guilt. Because it wasn't an accident, it was a tragedy. And even though I didn't do it intentionally, even though many other people might've done the same thing in my place, I was the one stopped at that crossing with the barrier arm down, I did what I did, and I'm at least somewhat responsible. The word 'accident' should be reserved for very few things; the majority of tragedies do not fall into that category. This building before me, the Lauría Health Clinic, is where they brought me that day, where they checked me out, where they treated my few cuts and bruises, and where, once I recovered from the shock, I began to understand what had happened. Although it was not yet clear to me that my life would be forever changed.

I resume my walk and I'm almost at Saint Peter's School when I stop. There's something missing. Before handing this envelope to my son I have one more place to visit. I walk a few blocks staring straight ahead, willing everything to stay out of my way, making sure nothing stops me. My phone rings inside my purse but I don't answer it. After about five blocks I turn towards the tracks, with apprehension, nervous. But to my surprise I don't find the barrier arm that I illegally drove past only to have my car stall and get run over by a train. Now, there's no barrier arm in sight. What was then a street-level crossing is now a tunnel that goes under the tracks, carrying drivers to the other side without any risk of collision. If by unfortunate chance a car happened to stall, no train would be able to run it over with a child trapped inside.

I let my gaze get lost in the darkness of that tunnel. It consoles me to know that the level crossing and the broken barrier arm no longer exist. I try to clear my mind of any thoughts that could pull me out of this moment. And I almost achieve it but then I hear the sound of an approaching train. It's a different sound, much quieter than what I remember from that afternoon. There's no blinking red light and no alarm bell, just the clattering that becomes louder until it's finally right in front of me, on top of the tunnel that is a dark hole of shelter from the train as it passes. First the locomotive and then one wagon after another. I follow the movement with my head, keeping my eyes on each wagon that comes until it's lost behind a building and then finally the entire train disappears and there's nothing left on the tracks. There's no barrier arm, no train, no car stalled in the middle of the tracks. No one had to decide whether or not to heed the faulty signals. Today, no one was in my place, because my place, where the tragedy occurred, no longer exists. I start to cry. And I'm filled with a deep relief. My contacts move out of place and everything is blurry. I'll have to rinse them with my saliva again. But I don't care about anything except the fact that the broken crossing signal is no longer there.

I walk slowly to Saint Peter's School. Mr Galván was worried. 'I went by the apartment and the doorman told me you'd left early, I was afraid you'd got lost.' 'I wanted to take one last walk before I go.' 'Oh, that's a good idea, let me know if you want me to show you around. Too bad you had to work all weekend, if not, I could've given you a better tour of the area. There are some nice places to see.' 'Yes, I appreciate the offer, too bad I had to work.' 'You don't have much time left, but let me know if you want to go anywhere else.' 'Sure, I'll let you know.'

Towards the end of the day I have a final meeting with Mr Galván that lasts about an hour. I explain how the evaluation process will move forward from here. How much time it should take. How he'll be informed of the results. If they're accepted as an affiliated school, they'll need to send a legal representative to Boston to sign the paperwork. 'Hope to see you there soon,' Galván says, and laughs. I smile too, but I don't say anything about the possible outcome of the evaluation. We've gone over everything and I'm getting anxious, thinking about how to tell him that I need to see my son – I won't say 'my son' but Federico Lauría, the history teacher – when Galván tells me he's called a staff meeting after school, with refreshments, so that all the teachers can say goodbye; it will start in a few minutes. I'm relieved by his words. It's a touching gesture and it also gives me the chance to see Federico and give him the text I've written. While I sit waiting in Mr Galván's office, I take the envelope out of my purse, I rest it on my lap and run my hands over it. If Mr Galván caught me caressing it – as he comes and goes talking about unimportant matters – he might think it was a wrinkled letter I'm trying to iron out. But he'd be wrong. I'm rubbing my hands over it not to smooth its creases but because of what the envelope contains: everything I have to offer my son and the hope that he'll accept it.

A few minutes later, Mr Galván leads me to the school assembly hall. Several teachers are already there, but my son is not one of them. Every time the door opens I look towards it hoping to see him. I'm disappointed by each new teacher who enters. I try to talk to everyone who comes up to me, as cordially as possible, to be Mary Lohan in spite of everything. After a while, Mr Galván introduces me to one of Mr Maplethorpe's sons, who's still a member of the board. I don't think I've ever seen him, I don't know if I ever crossed paths with him, twenty years ago. He's a man of about fifty and he looks vaguely like his father did back then. I'd like to ask him about John Maplethorpe, but Mary Lohan wouldn't be interested in the founder of the school, a man she's never met, so I simply say hello and add: 'A pleasure to meet you, your family has created a very fine school, congratulations.' He shakes my hand, thanks me for the visit, we have a brief, formal conversation, and then he steps away to talk to some other teacher. Meanwhile my son has yet to appear. I feel awkward holding the envelope, I move it from one hand to the other as I take a drink, tuck it under my arm to serve myself something on a plate and eat it with a fork. I try to balance everything so that nothing falls. But I don't set it down, I don't slip it back into my purse. I wait. Finally some of the teachers come over to say goodbye – 'It was nice to meet you' – and they leave. Everyone is beginning to leave. Mr Galván checks his watch and sighs, relieved to reach the end of the day and finally be free from that perpetual state of evaluation he's been submitted to over the past several days.

My son didn't come. He's not here and there are only five or six of us left in the assembly hall. A janitor begins cleaning. Finally, I pluck up my courage and ask Mr Galván about him. He's overly apologetic, 'Oh, I'm sorry I didn't mention it, I forgot,' and he proceeds to explain that Mr Lauría was the only teacher who had to miss my send-off. He tells me that Federico requested a last-minute leave of absence because he had to travel to some town in the province he can't remember the name of. He gets the attention of the secretary, who stands a few steps away talking to the last two teachers still left, and he asks: 'Where is it that Lauría's wife's family lives?' 'Trenque Lauquen,' the secretary answers, and turns back to her conversation. 'He had to go for some family emergency,' Mr Galván says. 'He's a very responsible young man, if it hadn't been something very important he wouldn't have gone, he'd have been here, of course.' And he repeats again that Federico was the only teacher who missed my send-off. I ask if I'll have the chance to see him again before I go. 'No, he won't be back until next week at the earliest,' he says, and he looks at me as if waiting for some explanation as to why I insist on seeing the only teacher who isn't there this afternoon. He may believe, incorrectly, that it's part of the evaluation. 'Is there anything else you need?' he asks worriedly. 'No, don't worry, Mr Galván, it's a minor issue,' I lie. I look at the envelope and I wonder what my son's absence signifies, why he left, why he confronted me the way he did only to disappear like that. Maybe he really did have a family emergency, but it seems hard to believe. I'm inclined to think that after finally facing me, he never wanted to see me again, that he'd got everything he had to say off his chest and he was now ready to close the book. He might not even want to read what I've written for him.

I smooth out the envelope one more time, I run my hands over it and wonder what to do with it now. Mr Galván checks the time and tells me that whenever I'm ready he'll drive me back to the apartment. I say I'm ready now and we walk to his car. On the way we talk about how I'll get to the airport and what time I should leave, which he says should be before five o'clock because of traffic. He offers to take me out for dinner but I say that I'm tired and I haven't packed yet. Mr Galván seems relieved at my response, neither one of us wants to sit through dinner together. When we get to the apartment he gets out to open my door, says goodbye one last time, thanks me, reminds me that I can reach out if I need anything as the evaluation proceeds. 'And I hope to see you soon in Boston to sign those papers,' he says again and laughs. 'I hope so too,' I say, and Mr Galván can't hide his satisfaction. I open the door to the building and I'm about to go inside but I stop just as he's about to get back in his car. 'Sorry, I almost forgot,' I lie again, 'would you be so kind as to give this envelope to Mr Lauría?' I say. I don't offer any further explanation, I don't say it's something we were working on together, or a publication that I thought might interest him, or any excuse at all. I just repeat the same words, maybe in a more imploring tone: 'Would you be so kind as to give it to him, please?' And Mr Galván says that yes, of course, and he asks: 'Is it urgent or can it wait until Lauría returns?' I hand him the envelope and answer: 'No, no, when he returns, of course, it's not urgent.' Then I walk into the building and step into the elevator as terror and hope engage in hand-to-hand combat inside me. I'm terrified that Mr Galván might be overcome by curiosity and open the envelope but hopeful that he's a trustworthy person – even if he thinks he's the sexiest man alive – and he'll make good on his promise.

I take out my contacts and place them in their case, I put on my glasses, pack all my clothes except for what I'm going to wear on the plane. I check the drawers, the bathroom, the desk to make sure I'm not leaving anything. And when everything is ready I begin my final task. I find an old newspaper at the back of the kitchen cabinet, I rummage in my purse for a box of matches, I take a wooden footstool from the office, and I go out onto the balcony with all of my equipment. I roll up a few newspaper pages and then set them on fire like a torch. I stand on the footstool and place the lit torch inside the hole in the moulding over the balcony. The lack of oxygen snuffs out the fire and black smoke swirls around the edge of the roof. I light my torch again. I repeat the same process several times, discarding the torch and making a new one when it gets too small. Until, finally, a little bat flies out of the hole and disappears into the night. Quickly, I ball up all the newspaper that's left and I shove it into the hole to fill it up, pressing it in tight to make sure there's no free space. So no bat can get in. So that the doorman won't pour poison inside to keep the next guest from being bothered by its droppings.

I light a cigarette and lean against the railing to look out over that city for the last time. I wonder where my son's house is, if it's nearby, if he's really in Trenque Lauquen or if he's here, hiding from me. I take a deep drag and then snuff out the cigarette. I ask myself whether hope will win out, whether Mr Galván will give my son the envelope without reading its contents. Without letting it get lost in some forgotten corner of his office.

But I tell myself that he will, that today's a day for things to go right. That just like that bat was lucky enough to escape that smoke, escape what could've become her tomb, my little luck will ensure that my text gets where it needs to go.

Even if no one reads it; that would be luck of another order.

Boston

I returned to Boston, to the house where I lived with Robert and that's now mine. We were never legally married, I never divorced Mariano and was afraid that when I tried to marry Robert the license wouldn't be approved and would only serve to bring up that past I didn't want to return to. But when we found out the cause of his unexplained stomach pains – cancer – Robert arranged to have everything he owned moved into my name. 'That's one good thing about this disease, it gives you time to put things in order. Even though you know the end is near, you can still do little, everyday things. Like someone has turned over an hourglass and we have to watch the time we have left slip away before our eyes. This illness is shit, but at least it gives you time, the sand slipping away, letting you know you're going to die. A heart attack doesn't do that.' And when he'd said he was 'taking care of things', I thought he was talking about the house, the bank account, the little cabin at the lake, even my job at the Garlik Institute. Now I know he was also talking about the trip to Argentina, about sending me to evaluate Saint Peter's School so that I'd have the chance to return to that place I'd run away from and to maybe repair some of my damage. That is assuming I agreed to go and assuming some damage could be repaired: factors beyond his control.

I've been back for several weeks now. Back to writing by hand in my notebook. I title the first text: 'Logbook: the Return.' I change the title of the text I wrote for my son, crossing out 'Why' and calling it instead: 'The Kindness of Strangers.' Followed by a note: 'Printed text written for Federico Lauría, typed copy of which can be found in my Word files.' Then I draw a line and put down: 'Boston'. Because Boston is my home now. I flew to New York and from there travelled by train, over four hours, to get here. I feel a sense of belonging here among the modern buildings contrasting with the elegant homes from another century, the streets and parks full of students and squirrels. Here, I know how to get around, where to find the best fruit in town, where to buy flowers and nice chocolate, where to see a good doctor, where to sit and watch the sunset, to read a book, to cry without anyone seeing. In Boston, everywhere I want to go is within walking distance. And I'm thankful because I like to walk, to feel free, to avoid sharing transportation with people I have nothing in common with besides the route we're all following. Boston, also, is Robert. And that gives the city an importance that no other city I'll ever live in will ever have, if I ever decide to leave here.

That's why, because this is my city, because I'm from here, I'm surprised to discover when I return from Argentina that I'm suddenly bothered by something I'd hardly noticed before: the cold. It's not that I'd never felt cold, no one who lives in Boston can avoid feeling the cold, it's one of the city's distinguishing characteristics. But for the past twenty years I'd never paid much attention to it, I wasn't affected by it, I accepted it as a fact of life. If I felt cold, I simply bundled up, put on a hat, gloves, my warmest coat. But I never complained about it, I wasn't concerned with it. That's why today I'm surprised to hear myself saying 'It's so cold!' I can barely withstand these late November temperatures, a mere foreshadowing of the winter to come. I've spent many Novembers here – it's not usually the coldest month of the year – I've endured entire winters, but I never suffered the cold like this before. It's as if a huge block of ice were penetrating the soles of my shoes and seeping up to the top of my head. My face hurts, my scalp hurts even under my wool hat and my hands sting through my gloves. The entire city is prepared for the cold: the homes, transportation, bars and coffee shops are all designed as warm havens to provide shelter from it. But the streets are another thing entirely. And despite the temperature, the city doesn't stop, people continue to come and go. I look right and left and see that almost everyone around me is young. 'The Athens of America', some people call Boston. The city of knowledge, of universities, of education. I walk around and I ask myself: do people care about education? Here or elsewhere. No one would admit they don't think education is important. But the budgets for it represent the tiniest portion of GDP, subsidies are getting smaller and smaller, educational quality continues to decline. Sometimes when I stop to think about these things I feel like I'm Robert, that I'm speaking for him, saying the things he would say if he were here. When he was here, I wasn't worried about these kinds of things. I listened to him complain, get angry, celebrate progress but also mourn what had been lost. We had conversations about it but it wasn't my battle, it was his. Education was Robert's thing. And Robert isn't here any more. I could allow it to fall out of my life, let it become just one more of the many issues I'm interested in, the field I choose to work in. But Robert left me not only a house and some money to support myself for the rest of my life, he also left me this legacy. Boston, even now, is still a city that values education, a place where everyone wants to study. Young people from all parts of the world flock to its schools and universities. Boys and girls flood the city. And even though I always knew that, today I suddenly see them. Like with the cold. I see a Boston full of young people in motion. They're all around me, marching to and fro in front of me, behind me, beside me. Lugging their musical instruments from one end of the city to another, their books, their video cameras, the pages they need to study. I watch a young man a few steps ahead of me. I can only see his back, his hair, the way he walks. It could've been Federico, a few years back. I wonder who his mother is, if she's nearby or far away. The majority of students who come to Boston live alone, or with friends. Their mothers stay behind in other parts of the country or the world. But they're available for a phone call, an occasional visit, willing to send them money if they need it, sitting in the audience at their graduation ceremony. These mothers, even though they're far away, are present. I wasn't present when Federico was in school, I wasn't there when he graduated. I'm sure his father was there, maybe Martha, his cousins, aunts and uncles, but not me. I'd have liked to know Federico as a student, to have him tell me what excited him, what bored him. To help him study when he had to pass a final for a class he was struggling with. What was the subject Federico most enjoyed? Which did he hate? Which course did he have to retake to pass? Today, as I walk this city, I long for something that was left behind in the past: to have been present, pouring hot water for his yerba mate as he studied all night. I didn't allow myself to wish for it at the time, I didn't dare, it didn't belong to my world of possibilities. Today I do wish for it, to have been there to pour hot water for my son's yerba mate while he studied. Or did he drink coffee? I have no idea whether my son drinks coffee or mate. I don't know whether he preferred to stay up all night cramming for exams or to wake up early in the morning and study all day. His father was a night owl, I preferred the day. Which one of us does Federico favour? I know almost nothing about my son's habits. But I now know a lot more than before going back to

Temperley to evaluate Saint Peter's School. I know what his face looks like at age twenty-six. I know he chose to study history. I know he's married and has a daughter. I know he remembers all the tiny details of that day our car stalled in the middle of the tracks. And that he's been writing down those details ever since. I know he was raised by Martha. That he wasn't happy in that family. I know that for many years he hoped for some news of me, some explanation of why I left him. Maybe now he finally has his answer, if Mr Galván handed over the envelope I gave him for Mr Federico Lauría and he, my son, decided to read what was inside.

I know very little about my son, but much more than I knew a few weeks ago.

I also know more about myself.

I know that after two decades in Boston I now feel the cold that was always present. Today, it bores into my bones as if it were the first time I were experiencing it.

And that I live in a city not only full of squirrels but also of young students. Suddenly, I see them.

Saint Peter's acceptance isn't decided by me alone. I merely filled out a series of forms with the preliminary results for the evaluating committee to consider. And I put forward a recommendation letter. Although they have yet to make their final decision, based on my experience at other schools and the additional information the committee asked me for, I'm certain Saint Peter's will soon be among the Garlik Institute's affiliated schools.

This period between the interviews in Temperley and the decision on Saint Peter's acceptance feels like life is hanging in mid-air. I resume my classes but I can't concentrate on the students. I've forgotten all their names, which has never happened to me before. I try to create a legend made up of cards with photos of each of them. I study the faces and names at night but it doesn't help. I tell myself that as soon as I can get Saint Peter's and what it means to me out of my mind, I'll turn back into Mary Lohan, the Spanish teacher, Robert Lohan's widow. Over time, Marilé will go back to being merely a dull pain I walk around with, no longer so vivid and alive. And María Elena Pujol will remain hidden away inside me, the secret underpinning of everything I am.

I walk around the house and I think that only now – after having travelled to Argentina – am I finally aware that Robert is no longer here. I go into a room that still smells like him and for a second I think I'll find Robert behind that door, doing up his shoelaces, reading a book, knotting his tie. Robert will look up, stop what he's doing for a second and say to me: 'How is my woman damaged doing today?' And I'll say: 'No new damage to report.' And we'll both smile. But that's not what happens, because I open all the doors and every room in the house is empty. At first, losing the person I'd shared the last twenty years of my life with seemed unreal, like his absence couldn't possibly be permanent, as if he might suddenly return from an unscheduled trip or wake up from an induced coma, come home, put the keys in the lock and I'd see his clumsy six-foot-six frame walk through the door. But it's been almost a year since his death and Robert is never coming home from any trip, he's never waking up. And his absence is now something I feel in my bones, like the cold that bores into me. And I try to accept that even though the house smells like him, his absence is not temporary, Robert is dead.

I'm still in contact with Saint Peter's School. But I haven't had any news of my son. A few days back I got up the nerve to ask Mr Galván about Federico in the postscript to an email updating him on the progress of the evaluation: 'P.S. Were you able to give the envelope to Mr Lauría?' To which Mr Galván responded: 'Yes, Mrs Lohan, the envelope made it to its destination.' But beyond my question and his response, which comprised no more than three lines, there's been no further news of Federico. I look back at the files with the names of the teachers and I realize that in the personal information section we don't even ask for the interviewees' emails or phone numbers. I'm surprised, disappointed, but I understand. There's no reason we'd need to contact them after the interviews, any contact should be made formally through the school. I don't know if I would've written to him even if I had his email address or called him if I'd had his number, but having that information would at least mean the possibility was there. Now I can't contact him without asking Mr Galván and I can't do that without offering some concrete explanation, telling him what I didn't tell him when I gave him that wrinkled envelope containing everything I never said to my son.

A few weeks later, Saint Peter's is formally accepted as an affiliated school. The evaluating committee informs me that they just barely squeaked by but that they met the minimum requirements needed. They asked me to follow up with the school on what they needed to do to finalize the process, who better than me since I went there and met them in person. I called the director of Saint Peter's to give him the good news and from the other end of the line came Mr Galván's euphoric voice saying: 'I knew it, Mrs Lohan, I knew it.' I told him I'd be following up with the more bureaucratic details by email, organizing the dates for their representative to come and sign the agreement, making the travel arrangements, obtaining the required information and documentation. I ask who would be representing Saint Peter's School on the day of the signing and Mr Galván proudly responds that he would be thrilled to do it. He tells me that he's very happy with the outcome and I give him my sincere congratulations. Over email, we finalize the details of his accommodation and I help him decide on some other places to visit since he's planning to stay a few extra days. From the questions he asks me – 'Is it worth going to Quincy Market, like everyone says? Is one whole day enough to see it or do I need two?' – I can tell that Mr Galván is almost more excited about his trip to the United States than he is about Saint Peter's passing the evaluation. I don't hold it against him. Robert would've been annoyed at his attitude, but I have to admit that Mr Galván has grown on me, he's a character, to be certain, but he's good at his job, he brings to it the kind of passion that Robert thought important, and at the same time he never fails to enjoy himself. But, most of all, I think it was that Mr Galván turned out to be the kind of man who will deliver an envelope to the person you ask him to.

I reserve a hotel room for him, I organize his schedule – arranging some meetings at the school as well as a few social events for our newest affiliated director – and I make sure I can be there to pick him up from the airport myself.

I'll be there to get him, in a few days, very early in the morning. But even though I like him more than I did when we first met, I won't talk to him about the flight or the weather, not even if a silence longer than twenty-three seconds falls between us.

Four days before Mr Galván's visit, I receive an email from him. It doesn't surprise me to see his name in my inbox, we've been exchanging frequent messages over the past several days. But this message is different. All of a sudden, he changed the subject of the email from 'Saint Peter's Contract Signing', to 'Change of Plans'. I open it. The tone, from the first line of greeting, is different. He says: 'Dear Mary', whereas in the previous emails he always greeted me as 'Mrs Lohan'.

From: Fabio Galván
To: Mary Lohan
Subject: Change of Plans

Dear Mary:

I will try to be brief, but I owe you some explanations.

I won't be able to travel to Boston. And despite the fact that I very much wanted to make this trip, I don't mind giving up my spot.

When Mr John Maplethorpe asked to schedule a meeting with me, I was very surprised. In all the years I've been at Saint Peter's I've met with his sons a few times, but never with him.

Of course I agreed.

He didn't come alone, he was with our high school history teacher, Federico Lauría. They have had a close relationship all these years, I'm not sure if you were aware. Mr Maplethorpe has been his mentor in many ways, and the person who transmitted to him his passion for history.

The two of them told me what happened twenty years back. I had no idea about the incident, being new to the area.

Maplethorpe explained that, given the circumstances, he felt that the best person to travel as representative of the school would be Mr Lauría, your son. And I was in complete agreement. I'll have to find another excuse for the Garlik Institute to invite me to participate in some other event! What do you think?

I should point out, because you might be interested to know, that Mr Lauría made this request very humbly. He did not use his relationship with Maplethorpe to exert pressure at all but simply because the former director was the best person to explain the situation to me. I admired your son's courage.

We've expedited the process of designating Federico as legal representative of the school so that he may sign the agreement. Everything is now in order. I wish you the best of luck. I wish us both the best of luck.

Lastly, I'd like to ask if you could transfer my hotel reservation into Federico Lauría's name and to let you know that he'll be travelling with his wife and daughter, so that you may prepare for the family's arrival.

I hope to see you again in the not-so-distant future.

Respectfully,

Mr Fabio Galván

My son is coming.

With his wife and his daughter, my granddaughter. I'm paralyzed. My heart is beating so fast and so hard that I'm afraid it might stop dead. This time I don't cry, there are no tears. I don't tremble. Just this uncontrollable pounding in my chest that echoes through my body. I try to calm myself. I read Mr Galván's email over and over. I memorize it. I try to picture being reunited with my son, imagine what he'll say to me, what I'll say. I know if he decided to come it's because he read what I wrote. I know that if he made the decision to travel here we're going to have a lot more to talk about than work and we'll see each other beyond the formal professional meetings. But I don't know if he's less angry at me than he was before or more so. I don't even know if he ever was angry. Or how angry. Each person reacts differently when the abyss suddenly opens up at their feet, they know they can't take another step because they'll fall in, but the options, the different ways around it, are often very different to what they imagine when they're peering over the edge. I left, I left my son and sealed myself up hermetically. Another person, in my situation, might have chosen a different route. The response to each abyss is personal and unique. I don't know what his was. My son might feel anger, rage, even hatred, but maybe also disappointment, sadness, shame. I don't know which of those emotions might win out over the others. I don't know what he feels today. I only know that he's coming to Boston to see me in a few days, that he read what I wrote. And that I'm going to pick him up at the airport.

I go out for a walk around town. Despite the cold so sharp it slices into my face. I feel the need to be in movement. I fear that if I remain still, the hours until it's time to go to the airport will stretch out and become endless. I cross a park. A squirrel runs right past me, and then another. I look up and wonder if I'll ever see a little bat in this city. I look back down across the park. A few yards up ahead sits a piano. Anyone who wants to can come up and play it. Probably left over from the Play Me, I'm Yours exhibit that last year flooded the city with pianos decorated by artists: at bus stops, parks, subway stations, random side streets. The entire city overrun with pianos waiting to be played. Or maybe this piano was always there and I just never noticed it. Every day since my return, I've discovered things that were right in front of me all this time but that I couldn't see before. The cold, the young people, a piano. Two girls walk past, they stop, one of them plays a few chords and they move on. I sit down on a bench nearby. A boy stops in front of it, sets his backpack on the ground, and plays a melody I don't recognize. And then another song. And a third. Every once in a while he makes a mistake, tries out a key that isn't the one he was supposed to play and then he starts the piece over from the beginning. A girl comes up, he greets her, and they leave together. The piano is left alone, I watch it from a distance, I'd love to play it, but I don't know how. I wonder if I'd be able to play it anyway, if I could just walk up and play any key, with any finger, without expecting to hear anything besides the sound it makes, then the next, letting myself be surprised by the music. Just that, pressing a key and waiting for the sound. And I'm about to do it, I'm about to get up from the bench and walk over to the instrument when another boy stops in front of it. I feel relieved, I sit back down and wait for this other person to do what I don't know how to do, or don't have the courage to. The boy is carrying an instrument case that looks like it probably holds a trumpet. He sets it on the ground, under the piano. He sits. He bends down, rummages in his backpack, and takes out a piece of paper. It's sheet music and he props it above the keys. The first chord rings out as he begins to play. This time, to my surprise, what follows is a melody I recognize, 'Fuga y misterio', by Astor Piazzolla, although the boy plays a different arrangement that doesn't always line up with the melody I have in my memory. I close my eyes to better appreciate the sound of each note, each chord. I remember my father teaching me to listen to Piazzolla. I remember the day I made Robert listen to him for the first time. When I open my eyes I see that several young people have gathered around the piano, in silence, to watch this impromptu street performance. I wonder if those young people know who wrote that melody or if they're simply enjoying it 'because it's the prettiest of them all', as my father said.

I'd like my son to be here. I'd like to bring him to see this piano that sits waiting in a park in Boston for someone, anyone, to pull music from it, any music at all. For the first time, I allow myself a wish that includes my son in the present tense, a situation that is possible. Not a wish to change the past, which is impossible. I can't pour hot water for his mate as he studies for his history degree. But I can wish for him to play this piano. Because my son, maybe, when he gets here, might go for a walk around the city with his wife and daughter, might cross this park and stop in front of this piano.

Maybe he'll play it, if he knows how.

And maybe I'll be there to hear it.

The day before Federico's arrival I receive an email from him. And a few minutes later, a second email.

The first one reads:

From: Federico Lauría
To: Mary Lohan
Subject: Signing of Contract

Dear Mrs. Lohan:

Tomorrow morning I will arrive in Boston.

I will be replacing Mr Galván as representative of Saint Peter's School for the previously scheduled meetings and the contract signing.

Sincerely,

Federico Lauría

I finish reading it and a strange sensation courses through my body. The email doesn't say anything bad, but Federico acts as if his trip to Boston were exclusively for work, placing a distance between us that would be correct if it weren't for the fact that he's my son. But he is my son. And then all my daydreams about his visit darken, become jagged. I no longer have any hope of seeing him play the piano in the park.

I try to calm myself. I pace around the house trying to decode that message. I think about Robert, about what book he would hand me in this moment. I tell myself that he'd come over to me, without saying a word, carrying a glass of wine and *A Lover's Discourse: Fragments*. He'd hand them both to me, I'd read the title and ask him what it has to do with me. And he'd respond: 'Between mother and child is a lover's discourse to be decoded, the first of them all, the one by which we measure all other messages.' That's what he said when he lent it to me the first time. 'In trying to decode another person's discourses we often make grave mistakes, filling the voids with misinterpretations of what a person said,' he told me. And I thought about my mother's absences, my father's silences, the look in Mariano's eyes, Federico's, 'Everything's fine, Ma.' My absence these last twenty years. My silence. I know, I know the error that decoding implies, and that that error can cause suffering. But I can't help myself. I imagine possible scenarios. I search for clues in each of his words. Barthes would tell me not to, Robert too. But I keep searching for coded messages that I can't decipher. Because there are none. That email says only what it says, that he will arrive tomorrow and that he'll be there to sign the contract. It means nothing more than that. And this is confirmed when a few minutes later a second email arrives in my inbox. One that starts directly with the body of the message, without a greeting, maybe to avoid having to name me – I continue decoding – to avoid choosing a name: Mary, Marilé, María Elena. I discard the notion that 'Mamá' might even be an option. My son wouldn't call me that.

From: Federico Lauría
To: Mary Lohan
Subject: Trip

I'll be there early tomorrow morning. I'm coming with my wife, Ariana, and my daughter, Amelia.

I read your text. Ariana read it first. I asked her to look at it and tell me if I should read it or not. Her eyes filled up with tears when she saw the photo you sent with it, my photo. Then she read it. When she finished, she gave it to me without any comments other than 'Yes, read it'. So I read it. Beyond random chance, or that little luck you talk about, we can thank Ariana for this reunion. She was always bothered by the resigned way I talked about my past. Ever since we first met she's asked me questions I didn't know how to answer. And she was shocked that I hadn't asked myself those questions all these years. I showed her my text, the one I gave you that last day. Even though when I showed it to Ariana it wasn't yet complete. Those final questions about why you left were missing. She brought it to my attention and I realized I'd always wondered, I just didn't have the words to express it. Why. But that unasked question: 'Why did you abandon me?' was always there, along with the possible answers. And with them the sense of guilt they caused in me as a child. A child can't separate themselves from their mother's decision to leave and never come back. A child feels that they must've done something to make that happen. And maybe I did, maybe not in the way I thought but in some different way, which is what Ariana helped me to see. Why didn't I search for you once I was able to, when I was old enough? Why did I let you continue abandoning me up to now?

After our daughter was born Ariana became even more insistent. She handed me the tiny baby in the hospital so I could hold her for the first time and she said to me: 'Now that she's here, now that you know what it feels like to have a child, what could possibly make you abandon her?' 'Nothing,' I answered immediately. She just looked at me. 'Nothing,' I repeated. 'Or something too terrible,' she said. 'From everything you've told me, up to the time you were six years old, your mother seemed like a woman who would only abandon you if something truly terrible happened. I believe that little six-year-old boy over your father or Martha. Or anyone else who tried to fill in the story. Find her and ask her.' 'Where do I find her? Give me her number and I'll call her,' I said sarcastically. Ariana didn't answer that day in the hospital, but as soon as we got home she started looking for you on social media, asking relatives and neighbours who were horrified when she mentioned you – my father almost stopped speaking to her – even searching different newspapers from around that time. Nothing.

Until one afternoon I stepped into the office of Mary Lohan and I saw your freckle. I didn't want to see it at first. I left there shaken, but totally denying the possibility that you could be who I thought you were. I told Ariana. She said to me: 'It's her.' 'How do you know?' I shouted, annoyed at her constant optimism. 'Because you know it. Take a look in the mirror, look how you're shaking. Look at your eyes. It's her, you're telling me it is.' So I wrote out that entire text I'd been working on for years, adding in those questions. I didn't sleep all night. I waited up until it was time for our meeting. And I took it to you. That's as far as I could go. Then I fell apart, I slipped back into a sadness I thought I'd defeated. I couldn't move. Ariana offered to go and see you herself but I wouldn't let her. She respected my wishes and she said: 'You'll see her eventually.' 'She's leaving on Tuesday,' I answered. 'Tuesday doesn't matter, you'll see her.'

Sometimes you're lucky enough to meet someone who brings out the best in you and the worst seems to disappear. It happened to you with Robert, who I only know from your text. To me with Ariana, who you'll get to meet soon. And with Maplethorpe, who in a way kept me standing until she got there. I'll tell you that part of the story later.

I wanted to send you this message before I saw you, because we'll have so many things to talk about when I get there. But I wanted to tell you some things in private – like for example how important meeting Ariana and having a daughter with her has been to me – so that when you meet them you'll already know what they mean to me.

We'll be there tomorrow.

I also rely on the kindness of strangers.

I know what it's like to be surrounded by people and still feel alone.

Federico

I'm at the airport waiting for the representative of Saint Peter's School. Waiting for my son, my daughter-in-law, and my granddaughter at Logan – which sounds ridiculously similar to Robert's last name, the name I now use. I hope I'll be able to spot them among all these people. Their flight is on time. A woman stops in front of me to answer her phone, I ask her if she came in on their flight and, annoyed that I've interrupted her, she says yes. I look at the passengers' luggage tags as they pass and several of them were on the same flight. A flight with a connection in New York that I would've suggested they exchange for a train ticket, if I'd had the right to make such suggestions.

I'm confronted with my reflection in a window. I straighten my skirt, button my sweater. I want to look nice. I spent a long time this morning deciding what to wear. I didn't want to show up dressed all in black, as I usually do. But I didn't want to wear something too bright; I tried on a red dress I wear every once in a while, but it didn't feel right. I ended up choosing an indigo skirt that Robert gave me the last Christmas we spent together. And the white wool sweater with purple embroidery I usually wear with it. Robert always said the outfit made me look younger: 'Today my woman damaged looks like a little girl.' I want to be younger. I want someone to give me back a piece of the twenty years I've lost. But that's not possible. There's no lost and found where I can go to claim those missing years. All I can do now is try not to waste a single moment from now on. I can't let any more time slip away, I have to grab it and hold onto it.

I play with the beaded necklace I'm wearing, a necklace with lots of twists and turns, I move it from side to side, I grip it tight like I imagine a devout Catholic might grip a rosary and a nonbeliever might hold onto a good luck charm. Today this necklace is my good luck charm. I rub it for good luck, brushing it across my collarbone.

There are fewer people now rolling their suitcases through the door, which I never take my eyes from. Until only a random straggler comes out every once in a while. I'm overcome by the fear that my son might've changed his mind, that he regretted his decision at the last minute and never got on the plane that was supposed to bring him here. I ask a man walking past what flight he came in on and he names another airline, another city. I stop the woman behind him and she says the same. I've almost lost all hope, convinced myself that there was never any possibility for a future involving my son and a piano in a Boston park, when finally Federico appears rolling two suitcases with an pushchair lying across the top of them. A few steps behind him comes the person who I imagine to be his wife with the baby in her arms, carrying a bag and a backpack. I press the beaded necklace into the knot that's formed in my throat and I make an effort to keep my eyes from filling with tears. I need my contact lenses to stay in place, my sight to remain unclouded, I need to see clearly even if it's through these brown eyes that no longer feel like mine. Federico walks towards me, stops in front of me, and says: 'Hello.' And I respond: 'Hello.' He doesn't give me a kiss or a hug. He doesn't even say my name. But a moment later – after an instant that feels endless – my son smiles, and turns around to introduce his wife. 'This is Ariana,' he says, and Ariana gives me a hug and a kiss on the cheek as she squeezes my shoulder with her free hand and pats my back. Then Federico says: 'And this is Amelia,' pointing to the baby in her mother's arms. My son looks at the baby and repeats her name, stretching out the vowels of each syllable: 'Ahh-mee-lii-aa,' and the baby laughs with a devastating joy. Ariana smiles and says: 'These two are trying to make me jealous. They can't get enough of each other.' I smile too. Then there's an awkward silence, that no one seems to know how to break, until my son's wife says: 'Well, let's go, we're in the way.' Ariana picks up the smaller suitcase, puts the stroller beside the other one that she gestures for Federico to take, and, lifting the baby up, showing her to me, says: 'Can you give me a hand with Amelia?' I'm paralyzed, staring at that little girl kicking her legs in the air as if she were pedalling a bicycle and I ask myself if I even know how to hold a baby. And I realize, in that instant, like a brutal revelation, that it's the same question I asked when Federico was born and I was left alone with him for the first time in the hospital: 'Can I do this?' Back then I didn't think I could, I didn't think I knew what a woman needed to know to hold a child. So I handed him over to his father. I handed him over. 'Can you give me a hand?' Ariana says again, and she holds out her baby to me. I return from that hospital in Temperley, twenty-six years ago, to Logan airport today. I return to my grand-daughter, and to my son. 'Yes, of course,' I say and I take a step towards her. The baby, still in her mother's arms, looks me in the eye and then turns around to meet Ariana's gaze. Her mother gives her an encouraging nod and that approval gives the baby the confidence she needs. Amelia smiles and stretches her arms out to me. I slip my hands around her and pull her towards me. She's light and warm. She's fragile. I'm afraid of hurting her. But I have to overcome my fear; I can't pretend I don't feel it but I can conquer it. I can act in spite of it, do what I have to do, what I want to do, with or without fear. I hold her close so she can't slip through my fingers, without squeezing her too tight. I hold her with one arm and support her back with the other. Amelia explores my face with her chubby hands. It's been many years since I felt such soft young skin against mine. Twenty years. She pulls at my cheeks, plays with my nose, gently slaps me. Federico says: 'Should we go?' I snap out of my trance and say: 'Yes, let's go.'

We start moving, Ariana and my son walking ahead. Each of them pulling a suitcase with their outside arms. And their other arms are wrapped around each other, hers around his waist, his around her shoulders. I watch them walk like that, in front of me, Federico's wide back, her small body some eight inches shorter than his. My son moves closer to her, leans down and gives her a kiss on the cheek. She turns to him, stretches up on her tiptoes and returns the kiss. The baby plays with my necklace – my good luck charm – moving it from side to side, from one collarbone to the other, every once in a while giving it a hard tug. Her skin against my skin as if we knew each other from some other place, some other time.

Maybe this is happiness: watching my son walk arm in arm with his wife, a few steps ahead, as I carry my granddaughter who pats my neck with her chubby hand.

Maybe that's all happiness is, an instant inhabited, a random moment in which words are unnecessary because it would take too many of them to describe it. To accept the instant in its pure, condensed form, without allowing language and its obsession with narration to dilute the intensity.

Time compressed and narration's failed attempts to expand it.

Happiness like an image to be contemplated in silence.

And a reunion.

This one.

ACKNOWLEDGMENTS

To everyone who read the draft of this novel and helped me by offering feedback:
Ricardo Gil Lavedra, Tomás Saludas, Lucía Saludas, Débora Mundani, Laura Galarza, Karina Wroblewski, Marcelo Moncarz, Paloma Halac, Patricia Kolesnicov, Jordi Roca.
To Julia Saltzmann, Pilar Reyes, Juan Boido and Gerardo Marín, who championed this novel from their first readings and transmitted their enthusiasm.
To my 'blended family' at Alfaguara / Penguin Random House who in their different roles and from their different locations contributed to and continue to contribute to the luck that *A Little Luck* has had in the world.
To Guillermo Schavelzon and his team.
To those who helped me but haven't read the book yet: Claudia Aboaf and Fernando Pérez Morales.
To my Facebook friends and Twitter followers who, unknowingly, cleared up some doubts that I had as I wrote this book, for example how long it's been since cars had automatic locks.

CHARCO PRESS

Director & Editor: Carolina Orloff
Director: Samuel McDowell

www.charcopress.com

A Little Luck was published on
80gsm Munken Premium Cream paper.

The text was designed using Bembo 11.5 and ITC Galliard.

Printed in March 2023 by TJ Books
Padstow, Cornwall, PL28 8RW using responsibly
sourced paper and environmentally-friendly adhesive.

MIX
Paper from
responsible sources
FSC® C013056
FSC
www.fsc.org